Published by 404 Ink
www.404Ink.com
@404Ink

First published in the UK in 2022 by 404 Ink.

Cover design: Fiachra McCarthy
Typesetting: Laura Jones
Proofreading: Heather McDaid
Co-founders and publishers of 404 Ink:
Heather McDaid & Laura Jones

ISBN: 9781912489503
ebook: 9781912489510

Printed and bound in Great Britain by Clays Ltd, Elcograf S.p.A.

NUDES

SHORT STORIES

ELLE NASH

NUDES

ELLE NASH

ALSO BY ELLE NASH

Gag Reflex
Animals Eat Each Other

FLUFFERS

YURI

PUKKAKI

MONEYSHOT

POV

SNUFF

For my daddy

CONTENT NOTE

FLUFFERS

IDEATION

IT BEGAN WHEN she moved in below their apartment, or maybe it began a week after when the boyfriend came downstairs to ask for a cup of sugar for a cake, or maybe it began a week after that when the girlfriend knocked on the door and asked for a cigarette and she didn't have any, so she said, "I'll go get some", when what she meant was, "Please come with me", because the town was new, because she liked the girlfriend's long, dirt-coloured hair. The girlfriend twisted the ends of that hair, patchy like sod in a hot yard that didn't take, the ends brittle from chlorine pools and heat straightening, bleached and ratty but silky at the roots where the natural colour was a deeper, more luxurious dirt colour. "I like Kools," she said to the girlfriend, and the girl walked with her up the street past the drainage ditch wet with grass, the night empty, the way small towns desert themselves after dinner, not a bright, living city, but potholed and sanctioned nonetheless, not a place where marijuana was legal. She touched the girlfriend's hand, and it was soft skin, young. "I meant Benson and Hedges," she said, remembering herself at the girlfriend's age. "I used to listen to punk music all the time."

NUDES

The girlfriend said, "What's punk music?" and she clutched her hand as they rounded the last corner to the liquor store, a cement-brick building with a neon American flag in the back window. "You know, anarchy? Fuck the USA?" The girlfriend was quiet, pulling the ends of her twill jacket over her fingers and glancing across an abandoned lot where a strip mall used to be, she bit her lip. "Why would you leave there?" the girfriend asked, touching her thumb and index finger together and bringing it to her mouth. "The place you came from."

"I don't mind keeping secrets with you. I have kept many secrets," she said, unbuttoning the jeans of incompetent clients three dates a week, most of them older, grainy-skinned and bitter, losing their wives to indifference. The flies near the dumpster murmured when a man slammed open the back door with an overstretched garbage bag.

"So, your secrets then," the girlfriend said. She didn't care if the girlfriend wanted her company for the free liquor or cigarettes since she wanted something from her, too, she said. This was how friendship worked as an adult: an exchange of goods or services for other goods or services. "I'm not sure what I want from you, exactly," she said. A new town is a chance to be whatever you want. She was happy to let the girlfriend make up stories of her so long as they were good. "But what about him?" she asked. She was itching for a cigarette now.

The boyfriend was soft-faced and had long lashes and small, cherubic hands. She'd noticed when she gave him the sugar. When he talked, his voice cracked. There was the girlfriend's mother, too, living with them—forty years old, curling tawny hair, drinking Natty Lights and asking if she could take her top off at the parties. No one ever minded. There were so many parties.

2

The girlfriend said he'd chased her once, the boyfriend stumbling through the apartment and then on to the balcony with a small, dull knife, and the girlfriend had yelled for someone to call the cops.

"He'd taken my phone," the girlfriend said. "My mom didn't do anything."

"Have you called the cops before?" she asked. "Yeah, but he becomes docile and they leave."

"Why would you stay?" she asked, but the wind had picked up by then, and she saw the man from the back door stare from the window, his nose trimmed with the hard red of the neon flag. She left the girlfriend at the side of the building and came back out with a handle of gin and a pack of smokes. A stiff, old lemon in her jacket pocket.

"Tell me about your clients," the girlfriend said. She told the girl about a man and woman who were in love with each other. They liked for her to teach them how to touch. Their touching was not clumsy or new but fearful, and she told the girl about the bright splotches of pink on the woman's body, across her cheeks and nose and down her breast. "She had ulcers in her mouth," she said. "Some chronic disease."

Another couple, another town, she used to let them tie her up and feed her GHB from a trinket-like vial. "I wanted to obliterate," she said, "any sense of self. They liked to pretend I was their daughter. I was sadder then, a lot like you." Then she said, "I'm sorry."

Back at the girlfriend's apartment, they were free to drink again and warming up. The girlfriend removed her jacket. The girlfriend's mother asked, "Are you a Hot Topic girl?"

NUDES

She shook her head and flicked a clear blue lighter beneath a cigarette, and the girlfriend's mother asked, "Are you a witch?" The girlfriend's mother took off her blouse, danced some, and opened the closet looking at her daughter's clothes. The girlfriend's mother tried them on, one at a time, each shirt smaller than the next. "There was a baby once," she whispered to the girlfriend. Before the misoprostol, she could only think about death or some form of it in her life. The girlfriend leaned into her on the couch and checked the time on her phone. "I don't think you should go to work," the girlfriend said.

The girlfriend's mother put a heavy arm around her and breathed into her ear. "I'm so glad my girl is here now, and not at the old house," the girlfriend's mother said, the old house with no plumbing or heating. "They kept shitting on the back deck, it just wasn't right." Torn linoleum, candled light. She placed the shot glass over the top of the gin bottle.

The girlfriend's phone thumped twice in her hands. "Don't answer it," the girlfriend's mother said. "He'll show up," the girlfriend said. The mother changed her outfit again, putting on a pair of her daughter's leggings and a crop top, the mother's bra peeking from the hem. Then the mother picked up a box of remaining beer and the bottle of gin and looked at her. "Shall we?" the mother asked, and they went downstairs.

In the apartment below, she locked the door and drew the blinds. She had no furniture, a blanket laid out on the floor, and a cardboard box for a table. She sat on the kitchen counter swinging her legs like a child. The girlfriend slipped off her moccasins and opened the kitchen window at the back, blowing pale clouds of cigarette smoke into the night. The mother unclasped her orthopedic bra. Bulbous, full breasts, which hung to the sides, areola as wide as her fist. She wanted to look; the girlfriend caught her trailing eye. "She is so fucking easy," the girlfriend said.

She liked the girlfriend's breasts, too. Her skinny ribcage, the way her sports bra compressed them close to her chest. Girls like that—their sharp chins pressing into her neck, the spidery way their fingers searched her body—it was how she wanted to be touched. Now she wasn't afraid of death so much as she was scared of running out of time. She worried about giving birth to an already dead child, or one who was alive and going to die. What it would mean to spend so much time obsessing over resources. The girlfriend looked bored, so she joked, "Sometimes the only thing in my stomach is cum, scrambled eggs, and coffee." She said, "Blow jobs are Ambien for bad boys." The girlfriend laughed, bright and soapy, and she liked the way her eyes ticked, gave way to surprise. They took shots and she asked about the boyfriend, asking again, why do you stay? Asking more, imagining the girlfriend plodding through the apartment, the boy with a weak chin and a kitchen knife in his grip. Why couldn't the girlfriend leave? The girlfriend pressed a thumb into the skin stretched on her jaw. She was embarrassed by how beautiful the girlfriend was, pink paint peeling from her fingernails.

"One time, in another city," she said, slowly caressing the metal lip of the vial in her pocket, "I might've gotten away with murder." It'd been the last time, with a man that looked like her father, the filmy gray of his eyes. His beleaguered breath, erratic and wheezing as he lay on the creamy foreign sheets in a room which overlooked an entire skyline on a river. She was tired of taking tiny capfuls of the drug to cope; its salty aftertaste like magnesium in her mouth. The man had downed his rum and Coke in a single sweep before collapsing. He convulsed once, then twice, rattling his teeth together, and then he threw up a rusty sludge. A wet, throttling sound came from his throat like he was choking. She'd panicked, pressing her hands into his doughy shoulders to roll him on his side. The girlfriend's eyes grew curious and there was a heavy rap on the door, breaking through the pop music. All three of the women turned their heads, the flirty dream dissipating. It was the first time anyone had knocked on her door since she'd moved in.

An older man with slicked-back George Clooney hair and straight teeth loomed through the crack at her. Behind him, the soft-faced boyfriend. "Leah needs to come home," said the older man.

"So what?" she said, but the mother had already slipped on her top and had taken the girlfriend by the hand, coaxing her back up the stairs.

The door shut, both the mother and girlfriend gone. She pulled the vial out of her pocket. It was enough to put a man in the dirt, but not a man and a boy. She didn't feel like running again, couldn't think of another town to move to. It wasn't enough to change things, she thought. She placed the murky vial inside the toe of one of the girlfriend's moccasins anyway, wedged into the fur lining. Death was a reminder that choice was a luxury. She tucked the shoes in her arms and opened the front door, into the cool night.

WHO'S AFRAID OF A FUNERAL PYRE?

MEG TOOK THE DIRT PATHWAY between her apartment complex and the strip mall where she worked part-time. A fire engine parked in front of building two, where Jodi lived. The lights flashed on the fire engine. Meg walked past, put her hands to her ears, and stiffened her body as though the sirens might wail. Two paramedics carried a yellow gurney up the wrought iron stairs. She stared, wanting to see who or what would be wheeled out. Her father had called it rubbernecking. He caught her staring at a crash as they passed it on the highway, once. "It's rude," he said. "Respect the dead." As a girl, she suppressed her urges but now sick curiosity compelled her. She'd never endured anything serious in her life, she felt, had never broken a bone, never even been stung by a bee.

Jodi stood outside the apartment with her mutt, Bella. Meg had a dog, too, a yellow lab named Cheese.

She'd gotten Cheese the year she dropped out of college and moved into an apartment by herself. Now she wasn't alone anymore and the dog was a good excuse to be outside. Bella sauntered leashless around the apartment grounds, as Jodi stood watching, a hand on her hip. Meg stopped and stood with her.

"What's going on?" Meg asked.

"It's the old man," Jodi said.

Blake, her next door neighbour, was always bitching about the old man falling, Jodi said. He could hear him curse, bang around; the heavy thud of his body on the floor above. Jodi said the last time Blake had a girl over, they could hear the old man crying in the middle of the night above him. Annoyed the piss out of him, Jodi said. She laughed, took another cigarette drag. "He told me it ruined the mood. The girl was no good for him, though, he said, so it was for the best."

They spent a few minutes speculating on the cause of death; heart attack, stroke, blood clot, blunt force to the head. Meg tried to remember what the old man looked like. When she first moved in, she stood in the middle of the street smoking cigarettes with Blake and Jodi and her boyfriend, Ben, watching the sky turn orange and violet. Everyone, except the old man, left their doors open in the summer heat, box fans blazing in the windows. None of their porch lights worked except for the old man's. The old man turned it on at 9 p.m. every night, blinding everyone. A silhouette of him appeared in the gold haze, asking Blake for a cigarette. It was always the same back and forth. Blake would tell the old man to shut the fuck up, to turn off his light or he'd go on up there and turn it off for him and the old man would yell back something like, "I'll do whatever I damn well please in this country of mine, of which I fought in a war I never asked to join, fought for you to have the privilege of smoking that damn cigarette in the street."

Then Blake would give the old man a cigarette. He never did anything about the porch light either. Blake was all talk, like the old man, like most of them.

Now, the old man's door was open. It was daytime, the porch light off. Meg still couldn't remember what he looked like. She wondered how long it would take before they carried him outside, maybe a long time. They got tired of waiting.

"Maybe we should go inside and smoke some weed," Blake said.

"Oh, you're here," Jodi said.

"Just got home from work." He put his hand on Jodi's shoulder, then walked past her to his door.

The smell of human waste collected in his carpets. Meg tried to ignore the dead roaches in the corners of the apartment, the plastic pucks of poison strewn about. Every time Meg saw a roach in her apartment she killed it instantly. It made her shiver to think of roaches skittering behind the cabinets or beneath the carpets; when she'd read online how to get rid of them, the listicle said if you were seeing them in the daylight, the brood was so overstuffed the roaches were hunting for food. Seeing the roaches piled up fascinated her. Like, what if she just gave up cleaning? It was a continuous game—finding the roaches, killing them, cleaning up their dead bodies.

Blake sat on his couch and opened the false wood top of his coffee table, revealing several glass jars of weed. As far as Meg knew, Blake lived alone. Sometimes a girl would show up, always a redhead, short or tall, carrying a duffel bag, a makeup bag, or a small dog, but a few weeks later she would be gone. If Blake was unhappy about their leaving, he never let on. Jodi would look gratified when the girls left. She'd cut Blake's hair, trim his beard. Sometimes Blake cooked dinner for Jodi, like

NUDES

venison steaks and fried onions, a repayment of sorts, Meg thought. Jodi's children, all girls, were grown and gone. Blake took a glass jar labeled Green Crack, picked a nugget out, and put it through a grinder.

Meg got up when Blake lit the bowl, and passed through Blake's bedroom to use the bathroom. There were holes the size of fists in the drywall, which she'd never seen before. The bathroom was equally filthy. Meg imagined herself as one of those girls waking up in the morning, doing her makeup in the fractured mirror. Blake's anger was simple and obvious. It was too impatient. She had spent much of her life living with angry men; her father had been angry, and now so, too, was Ben. It was what Meg expected. There are not many women who can live with angry men, Meg thought.

It wasn't all bad. Ben had a good heart. He treated small animals with respect, even spiders. And his intellect, his thought-fulness toward the nature of human behavior, was deeper than any person's she'd ever met. Other people were emotionally flat and less interesting to engage with. She figured them out easily, and as a result, got bored too quickly. That was what she could see in Ben, what no one else saw, like tectonic plates slipping beneath each other. He never turned his anger on her, just as her father had never turned his anger on Meg or her mother. He'd always get angry at other things, and it seemed that Meg's purpose on earth, as her mother's purpose on earth had been, was to witness this man's anger and somehow sieve him back into the world. It was a way for men like this to be normal, she thought—how they survived was bringing their anger home.

They took turns passing the glass pipe, shaped like a banana. Meg had the thought she should go home and let Ben know

10

where she was. She worried one day his anger would shift toward her. She took another hit; she didn't want to miss the firemen removing the old man's body from the apartment.

Jodi crossed her legs, leaned in close to Blake, and blew out smoke. "I guess his son will be showing up to take care of all the man's belongings. The man's a hoarder. Imagine they'll be sorting through lots."

When she got home Meg told Ben of the news of the old man, "That's the problem with people today," Ben said. "Nonchalantly dealing with death."

"Some funeral for a war hero," he added. Meg nodded.

"We should burn the apartment down," she said. "A funeral pyre."

Ben side-eyed her, but to Meg, he looked like he was contemplating the idea.

In the night, Ben's hand searched for her. The tenderness of his warm palm against her body was something concealed and uncertain. Later in the week, the old man's belongings were thrown from his bedroom window into a dumpster below. Newspapers, chairs, stuffed animals, broken lamps, computer monitors, CD cases, more newspapers. A few neighbours came by to examine the furniture that survived the fall. Meg pictured herself dead, the contents of her home thrown in the trash, strangers digging through it. Each person would pick out an item and smile as if they'd won a prize.

The smell of urine hit Meg each time she walked past the dumpster. Everything stank like urine now. She went home and Ben told her of all the terrible things happening in the world: genocides, famines, political corruption. He said, "What's the point in ever going to Paris if there's bulletproof glass around the Eiffel Tower!"

Meg listened to Ben while telling Cheese to sit. She put his collar on him and then his leash. Ben continued on his tirade. She stood at the door, fidgeting with the leash in her fingers, waiting for a pause in the conversation. Cheese turned in circles.

"I'm listening to you," she said, "but I'll be right back." She felt the heaviness of Ben's anger on her like an old coat. But when she left the apartment, she took the coat off.

The dog trotted alongside her as she walked up the street. The night was purple and loud with summer, the moon peeking like neon through the trees. Bella was out wandering and Cheese pulled on his leash and whined a little. Jodi's and Blake's doors were open but Meg couldn't see anyone. She pulled Cheese past where the fire engine had been parked, the spot now empty. Meg stopped and examined an old chaise on the curb, considered dragging it back to their apartment. A small craving tugged at her to take this haunted object, as though she needed a reminder that an object's usefulness far outlives its owners. She bent down to sniff it—that ammonia sting—and noticed a brown stain on the tan upholstery. The chaise would be useless to her. She thought perhaps she should burn it—set it on fire right in the middle of the apartment complex. Meg could lie on it, arms folded across her chest, and let the flames lick away the fabric of her coat.

JOAN JUMPS INTO THE SEA

A SMALL CHILD CAN SWIM through the veins of a blue whale. This was how I swam to you. They told me you were lost to combat, but I knew you were a fighter. On the third day of your absence, I walked to the edge of the wooden world, raised my hands to the sky and plunged into the water. A blue whale swallowed me in one gulp. Through each vaulted vein I swam, hurtled toward the canyon of her chest. With each long breath I crawled out and into the dark blue, squeezed around the corner of a ventricle, and pressed a restless hand, pale against the muted walls of meat. In the middle of the whale was a pulsing city with flesh that gave way like sand. It was there I found you, past the veins. In the canyon of a heart that wasn't yours.

BRITTANIES

SO HERE'S A LITTLE OVERSHARING. Me and Brittany, just friends. Meatsack was in love with her. Me and her, we partied a lot. But just friends. I never fucked around with her or anything like that. But something she would do, whenever I brought a girl around, she would step up and get possessive. That first party I took you to where we played poker for cigarettes, Brittany shows up and she started doing her thing, you know, and she did this a million times over where she was super possessive of me where it would be like, not a thing, but an implied thing. Anything she could do to suss out any kind of insecurity. You were the first girl who didn't balk.

After, we had to bail, so it was ... We had to bail, and then it was Tuesday when I hung out with her again, and she said, "Dude, that girl, she's fucking rad as fuck." She vouched for you. And that shit mattered later.

She ended up with Rayray. I don't think you ever met him. Me and Rayray ... so that was something else, too. Me and Rayray were really close because out of the two of us, we were the only ones who could drink that much. We shut everything down together. Then Meatsack went to work at his tattoo shop.

I was the guy who put in Meatsack for that. We used to do that shit. That's what got really weird. I don't know if you know about the killings in St. Louis ... the guy who set that bar on fire. There was a bar on Fourteenth and Crane, with a parking lot right there, and so where Fourteenth ended, that's where Crane jogged. It was off of that parking street connection. It was where Meeks, Fourteenth and Crane intersected. That was the bar Rayray owned. So that night, I left early. And um. I left early, Rayray called me, we went to a place called The Back Patio, and we partied there, and we bailed out, and we ended up sleeping on his couch. He lived off the I-55 exit that was just east.

We used to drive past it all the time. Brooklyn. The little crook that separates from everything else. So I slept on his couch, that's when that shit got burned down. Rayray thought I did it for three weeks after that.

Because I hated this son of a bitch named Aaron—it doesn't matter. Look. Dude ripped me off. I was super pissed. Why do I even remember this? It's bizarre.

Brittany ended up dating Rayray. Initially she was kind of weird about it. I was like, "No, no, he's a great guy, he just parties hard." We all did back then, drinking a lot, doing a lot of fucking coke. Brittany goes down, she seems like she could handle it. I don't know. There was a lot of animosity between me and Meatsack. He ended up falling in love with all kinds of girls. He was like way sensitive, too.

Shit, man. So this one time Meatsack was in love with the Brittanies, so ... what was her name. Brittany Smith. And there was Brittany Siebens. They were hot sisters. I don't remember. Maybe they weren't sisters. I remember the one girl, Brittany

Siebens. You know who I'm talking about? Black hair Brittany, and blonde Brittany. And blonde Brittany, he was all about her. And she liked me. I already told him, we got housed once and he got me drunk as fuck and he was like, "No, you're gonna tell me the truth." He passed me a shot and I was fuckin' bleary eyed and couldn't see shit and he was like, "I know you always tell me the truth when you're drunk." And I said, "Man, I'd never fuckin' lie to you." And he said, "Take that shot." So I took it, and he was like, "Do you have any intentions with Brittany? Siebens?" And I was like, "Nah dude, that's all you man."

And he was like, "Why? You don't think she's hot?" And I was like, "Yeah, she's fuckin' hot dude."

"But why?"

I told him, I was like, "Man, you saw her first dude, it's cool. You know. There's all kindsa females. It's cool. That's your female. You do what you gotta do."

And he was like, "That's why I love you." He grabbed my face and pulled it to him, and he was all slobbery, you know, he was like, "I love you." I remember it. It was a good day.

Anyway.

So uh, Brittany Siebens. One time, she called us, we were on a fuckin' mission, running shit up the goddamn fuckin' highway. We were goin' up to Firestone 'cause we had to sell some shit. And we doubled back because we got a phone call from her.

We come back, and she's, uh, she gives us an address.

I didn't fuckin' recognise it. So we looped into this apartment complex and we go in this fucker and like, I'm not kidding. It's a one bedroom apartment. On the couch is three dudes. I never seen them before in my life. Fitted caps, wife beaters, all this shit. And these guys are acting like they're fuckin' tough already. I said three guys, two of 'em. One of 'em stands up, you know what I mean? And he's already trying to fucking front on them. And I was like, "Wait man, calm down. He's just trying to see his sister. Meatsack's sister. That's what he's doing."

Anyway, so she comes out. She comes out of the fuckin' back room, right, and she's like bawling fuckin'… she's got eyeshadow running down her face and shit. Blonde hair tangled up. Meatsack grabs her, like some *Casablanca* moment, and just fuckin' kisses her in the goddamn living room. And the dude that's fronting on me, he looks at them. Looks back at me, looks at her, looks at me, so I just clocked him. I fuckin' clocked the fucker.

He hits the dirt. And then her boyfriend—yeah, I think that's who he was—he stands up, and grabs her by the arm, he rips her away. Meatsack turns and he grunts, "You're gonna let that female go."

Right, and it's funny 'cause he's short and fat. He don't care. I love that boy. He does a little of this, and that guy fuckin' decks him. He does one of these, he hits the guy with an uppercut. Pressure has left the cabin. Hits him so fuckin' hard. He does one of these, the dude spins around, lands on the couch. Soon as he hits the couch, this dude, that I already clocked right, he's turning back around. So I fuckin' hit him again. Brittany starts screaming, you know. She's like, "Gaaaahd, that's my fuckin' baby's daddy." Meatsack is already on top of him pounding out the motherfucker. This dude's already hit the floor, so I start kicking him. I saw one start running for the fuckin' door, so I grab that son of a bitch, I chuck him, fuckin' roll him. Soon as I roll him, Meatsack hops on him, hops on him, right. It's like hop on pop. I roll that bitch, he's like, oh shit, hits him.

As soon as he does that, he starts thinking ideas, I hit him instead. And it's like, it's just full blown. Me and him just pounding kids. Don't even know what the fuck is going on.

Just fucking wailing. Don't even know, man. Seeing red. Fuckin' hitting fools.

The point I'm trying to make in this shit, is we extricate the female, and we get in the car and we're driving away. She's fuckin' freakin out. "Dude fuckin' beat me, did this shit, gave me a black eye, one time he hit me in the arm, you can see right here there is the bruise." I didn't see the bruise so I punched it. And Meatsack is like, "Hey man, don't hit the female," and I'm like, "Alright, it's cool, whatever, it's just for fun," whatever, I dunno.

We get her back to the fuckin' spot and he's all kissy kissy, oh baby, we'll make it alright, he ends up fuckin' her, she ends up splittin'. But her sister moves in. When we saved her, her sister was like, I need to be saved. And him, being fuckin' white knight supreme, right, rescues all the ladies. So he's got like him, blonde Brittany, her sister, their friend, what was her name Sarah, I think, in the fuckin' cut, hanging out, twenty-four-seven, no rent needed. And it was this crazy trap house bullshit.

So we're up in this cut, fuckin', these females are there, shit's fuckin' weird. This is the night that I poured out the beer on the table, and I took the cat and used the cat to mop it up. So he goes, "Hey man, let's just play some Rock Band." And I said, "Man I don't wanna play any fuckin' Rock Band." And he said, "Hey, dude, don't even worry, we have some fuckin', uhh, Smashing Pumpkins." And I was like, "I love Smashing Pumpkins." And he's like "What white guy doesn't?"

I ended up singing to Billy Corgan, and everyone was really amazed because I can do a fantastic Billy Corgan. It's not very easy to stop up the nasal holes. Doing that shit, it's going great. So him, Brittany Siebens, and the fuckin' friend, they end up like moving on. You know? Into the bedroom. So I have to bail.

NUDES

I go home. And uh. I drive home drunk as shit, high as a fuckin' kite, hit that shit up. I remember, fuckin', ex-girly bitchin' about it. Her bullshit about like "You're rollin' in at four o'clock in the fuckin' morning. I have fuckin' class, why you gotta be fuckin' doin' this, who the fuck do you think you are." And me being like, "Bitch, go the fuck to sleep."

I play video games until 6 a.m. Pass out with my dick out. Shit's solid. Wake up. He fuckin' hits me up: "Man we gotta fuckin' hang out." Hell yeah, I'm gonna hang out because I wanna hear about what the fuck he got up to. We slam down to this place, where was it, it was Denny's in Maplewood right off the fuckin' interchange, got some eggs and shit, and I was like, "Yeah man what happened," and he told me, he said, "That's the first time I know what it's like to be fucked like a girl." And I was like, "What do you mean?" And he was like, "Man, she was like way aggressive, like, kept humping different parts of me, but not the parts I wanted her to hump, it was strange." He got completely taken away. He was like, "That's how I know what it's like." He was scarred.

I was like, "How is this not good, dude? You had, like, two ladies? Is that not fun?" He did not think it was fun. Swore the whole thing off and never wanted to do it again.

Brittany Siebens eventually ended up moving out and going back to that dude we fuckin' wrecked in his apartment. That shit triggered the shit out of him.

Because of that shit, we had to call Rayray to come help. He was pissed about that. So we both show up, hovering over Meatsack's shit, I brought Clamatos. What really happened was Meatsack was moving shit and me and Rayray are just sitting there drinking. Brittany Smith shows up, sees me, throws her arms around me, you know, cuz she's like, "Oh boy, you're here, you got coke, let's do this," etc etc, so you know what I mean, we start cutting the shit, and she sees Rayray and she immediately head-over-heels falls in love. Like can't even believe this boy exists. And I was like, "Meet Rayray." You know? Like, haha, match made in heaven. For the longest time too, like, when that shit initially kicked off, people were constantly, you know. 'Cause me and her, I would take her dancing, we did all kinds of shit. And forever, you know, I was like, we're friends, it's stupid, don't even trip about it. But when that shit happened people thought I would flip out. I was like, "Nah, man, she's not the girl I couldn't fuckin' get. I don't fuckin' want her. She's not for me."

It was clear. Super clear she's not for me. She's a special kind of crazy. She worked for him. Mm. Yeah, right up until she stabbed him.

They got into a fight. He raised his voice and she doesn't like that, so she stabbed the fucker, oh yeah, I remember this because I had to pick her up, and had to drive her back to fuckin' Mama's house, and then. Oh yeah. You got me in a fuckload of trouble over that shit, too. Like when you stayed the night. You have no idea. That cost me 260 fuckin' dollars. I don't think I ever told you about that.

YURI

CAT WORLD

ExxonMobil6 wants to put his fingers in my mouth until they wrinkle and turn pink. He wants to palm the thick cord of my trachea. He might even want to push against it, watch my face turn pale until the tiny egg of my vision blurs bloody like a video game victim: YOU DIED.

ExxonMobil6 tells me this in an AOL chatroom for people who cosplay as catgirls and catboys. My avatar is a peach coloured anime girl with white cat ears tufting out from her short dark hair. I drew a copy in art class after finding pictures of her online in her sailor fuku, with her large, wide green eyes, her white panties and thick crew socks. I love her white socks.

When Exxonmobil6 PMs me he asks A/S/L and I tell him 18/F/Florida because I've always wanted to live in a panhandle. But when he asks where in Florida I don't know what to say. I've never been. My uncle runs a charter ship out in Summer-land Key, so I tell him that.

NUDES

ExxonMobil6: the keys. must be nice living in a place like that.
dErAnGeDkItTy69: yeah lol
ExxonMobil6: how's the atlantic?
dErAnGeDkItTy69: what?
ExxonMobil6: the ocean. you live in the keys?
dErAnGeDkItTy69: oh yea

I tell him about going to the beach in bikinis with my friends, how we drink cold vodka from red cups and sit around bonfires cooking hotdogs and making s'mores.

"I would love to see it," he says. "You and your friends in your bikinis, spread-eagle."

I admit I don't know what spread-eagle means. "lol", he says. Just like that.

ExxonMobil6: send me a pic
dErAnGeDkItTy69 has logged off

At school, Mikaela passes me a note. *You get high?* I write back and tell her I used to (a lie), and I quit (also a lie) but I'd be interested in giving it another shot. I am interested in getting high, that's not a lie. I like Mikaela. She has a face like a Disney princess, hides her long hair beneath a Von Dutch hat and refers to herself as a hippie even though she's only fourteen, like me. Her front teeth are cartoon-rabbit-like. Tacked to my bedroom wall is a photo of her. In it, her eyebrows are half-raised beneath a baby-blue bucket hat. She's standing next to Ash, who moved to California halfway through freshman year. We were at our first dance at Ellet High. My mom had dropped us off. My parents were getting divorced. But like a lot of things, they'd only gone halfway, so my dad slept on the couch. He'd get home from work and we'd eat dinner on TV trays at the couch like always. After that, he'd watch news after while mom did the dishes like always. He'd have a drink and lie on the beige, itchy thing until he fell asleep, the TV blathering on. Mom, in her flowy silk robe, would ascend the stairs to her king-sized bed with its carved wood headboards like some fairytale queen.

One night I'd pulled an all-nighter to finish an essay and caught her sitting on the bed facing the open door, catatonic.

My dad slept facing the computer cart, a ratty blanket wrapped around his bare, hairy belly.

At school, Mikaela passes another note.

My family is a bunch of hippies, too, it says. *This Friday we're gonna come pick up sweet lil' you and fuckin party.*

"If you're going to spend the night, I need to meet Mr. Donahue first," my mother says. I cringe. I'd message Mikaela on AIM but she doesn't have a computer. The next day at school I slip her a note; she scribbles back to say her dad will meet my mom when they come to pick me up.

On Friday night, Mr. Donahue gets out of his truck and sweeps his brown shoulder-length hair back. He scratches his nose when my mom asks where they live then ferrets the hand back into his corduroy pants.

"Two streets down from the high school," he says. He scratches his nose again and sniffs. I lean out of the door and see Mikaela and her older brother Mason are in the truck. "Don't worry, hon," Mr. Donahue says. "She'll be safe with me."

My mom nods.

"Be back by ten tomorrow," she says. I squeeze into the backseat of the truck with Mikaela. The wind blows our hair back and she puts her hand on my thigh, curls her fingers into mine. The sun sets as her dad pulls into the parking lot of a motel with stucco walls and neo signage.

The room is already rented, their gym bags sitting in the corner. A bag of make-up and a stereo on a desk. I ask Mikaela if she lives here and she says it's just temporary. Her dad puts on The Doors and pulls out liquor and a little glass bong. I realise she's never mentioned her mother. We drink, and Mason asks me if I've ever kissed anyone. I think of Exxonmobil6. Mikaela laughs and says, let's fix that. The bass rattles helplessly through small speakers and she leans across the bed smiling with her rabbit teeth and I part my lips in expectation. She grabs my face with one hand, pries open my mouth with the other, and starts to lick at the empty space above my tongue. I feel Mason's hand tuck loose strands of hair behind my ear and hear the click of a digital camera.

In the catgirl chatroom I wait for Exxonmobil6 to log on. I want to tell him I went to a party. While waiting, I'm just watching an argument between random strangers unroll.

fabio_maximus: japanese cat girls are NOT AND never WILL be part of the furry fandom.
1. furries are anatomically designed more like animals, with muzzles, haunches, and animals paws, features that are more in line with animals. 2. Furries are not associated with otaku culture or anime. 3. (as a subset of 2.) some ppl really, really seem to be pretty interested in any intellectual contortion that can convince people they are into furries, as som ekind of insult, as opposed to cat girls just being like regular girls but hotter.
pinkfox: catgirls are popular with furries, ymmv

T99_34: its more like a spectrum honestly. The 'completely human with cat-ears' girl is, imo, really not furry. But there are fully furred cat girls and cat girls with some fur in more animallike, or 'furry' type places, if you will, with fullyfurred furries on the major end of the spectrum. Technically they are all furry. The appeal of any catgirl comes from the same underlying psychological reason people get into furries but some characters just reflect it far more or less than others.

potentspit: I've always wanted to suck on a cat girls tail i don't think that makes me into bestiality tho

GADE: furries have fur. catgirls do not have fur. furries also have more cat like qualities to their face.

ultimate_chicken: lizard or bird furries don't have fur. still furries.

After the party, every Friday until summer I lace my fingers with Mikaela's in the Bronco on the way to the motel expecting more of the same: the bite of rum her dad buys us, the crush of ice between our teeth. Each note we pass in school inches closer to affection: *do you like me?* I think I like you. *Do you wanna be my gf?* Sure, I'll be your gf. A dozen hearts and smiley faces flutter between us in origami fold. Her dad routinely leaves us at the motel and shows back up after 8 p.m. with a pocket full of change and crumpled dollar bills. He throws the change on the desk.

"Spange-ing," he says.

"What?" I ask.

"He stands on the corner with a sign, asking for money," Mason says. Her dad pays for another night, disappears to the car, comes back with a bong and a rum bottle. I watch Mason twist and turn the bulb of a meth pipe, the rock inside rolling like a hamster in a wheel, spitting into nothing.

NUDES

The next morning I wake on the bathroom's linoleum, cool squares against my sweaty cheeks. Without washing my face I swipe eyeliner over yesterday's eyeliner, take a Q-tip and dab at the smudges beneath my eyes. It's almost ten and everyone's asleep. I nudge Mikaela's dad awake, and he drives me home. On the highway I struggle to keep my eyes open, the night a pulsing memory.

"Your mom won't think it's strange it's just me dropping you off, right?" he asks. He wipes crust from his eyes.

"No," I say. "Thanks for the ride, Mr. Donahue. You can drop me at the end of the street if you want."

He scratches the rim of his nose. "My name is Bobby, by the way."

In the bathroom at home I peel off my shirt and look at my sunken stomach, my breasts too small for even a training bra. In the two-story house where my dad sleeps on the couch, the bathroom is cream tile with black grout. The faucets are brushed silver and the clawfoot tub is free of rust. Nothing smells of rotting wood. The only drugs in the house are cigarettes, coffee. I notice a small bruise on my side but can't remember where it came from. I think of Mikaela. Something in her laugh excites me. Her chest seems warm, hidden beneath loose tank tops. I wonder what her nipples look like, if they're tan like her wrists and neck. She has these eyes that slope down, hair almost the same shade as her skin. A mole on her upper cheek. When she laughs, her teeth look just like her dad's, just like Bobby's.

Eventually, Mikaela turns fifteen. School lets out and I walk in the heat until I see spots. Mikaela doesn't call for weeks. I sit in front of the PC for hours, my eyes burning out like lightbulbs. It's not Exxon's normal time but I've told him school is out so I'm waiting for him to show up. The problem is you find a place you think you might belong and want to violently wedge yourself into any open space warm enough to welcome you.

ExxonMobil6: my little neko
dErAnGeDkItTy69: *cocks head to the side, squints at your silhouette in the sunlight. my silky tail uncurls to greet you*
ExxonMobil6: you're not as graceful as other nekomimi, but thatsuffices. I dont want to have to takeyo u to the pound.
dErAnGeDkItTy69: please don't! *crawls up to you and nuzzles on your knee, waiting for your pets*
ExxonMobil6: *scratches the soft fur behind your ears* tell me about what you've been up to.

I tell him I'm applying to colleges, that I don't want to go to college but my parents are making me.

"Do you always do what your parents tell you to do?" he asks.

"No …" I say. "Not always." I type that I lick my wrist and wipe the top of my head with it, cleaning one of my catgirl ears. I send a kaomoji that looks like a devil face:

(((←~ (o `∇´)oψ

I tell him my parents are going on a second honeymoon, that they used to fight a lot but finally realised how much they love each other and decided to celebrate their love in Jamaica, all summer. I'll have the house to myself—the house on the beach, in the Keys. Exxon says, "I'd come visit you, but I'm nowhere near the coast." I ask him where he lives and he says, "College would be good for you. What do you want to study?"

I change my avatar from a catgirl with blue eyes to one with green eyes. The new catgirl still has short black hair, but instead of a schoolgirl outfit, she's wearing a black triangle bikini with white edging and her breasts are huge. Exxon has an anime avatar of a man with blonde hair, pointy chin and glimmering square glasses. I think of him as sophisticated and poised. I type to Exxon that I curl up at his feet. I type that I lick my paws, but my ears are pointed back. Exxon types that he scratches the soft patch of skin behind them. I imagine myself radiating warmth into his hairy legs. I imagine him as human, not as cat. Like an owner. When I don't purr, he asks what's wrong.

"I don't know what I want to study," I tell him. My tail moves back and forth but not in contentment, more like frustration. I tell him I want to study writing. I tell him how I imagine my future: living in New York City, writing poems. He sends me poems by Charles Bukowski and I write them all down in my journal. I type that my catgirl ears flick in a happy way. The gentle rhythm of our red text, blue text fills me with confusing, erotic need.

Exxonmobil6: will you ever send a pic?
dErAnGeDkItTy69: parents home. g2g. sorry.
ExxonMobil6: i thought your parents were on vacation?
dErAnGeDkItTy69: ╲(ー＿ー)╱ i know I said that …
ExxonMobil6: don't talk to me again until you send me one.
ExxonMobil6 has logged off

On July fourth, my dad moves out. It's been a week since Exxon has talked to me. Mikaela and Bobby and Mason come get me in the Bronco and a new person sits in the front passenger seat. I squeeze between Mikaela and Mason and look at the man up front, who introduces himself as Shawn. Down the highway, I watch the wind whip my face pink in the rearview. I don't want to ask Shawn to roll his window up. Car dealerships pass by, then the paper mill, red and green warehouses, the train yard filled with abandoned cars. What I like about cat world is that we type out our body language so it's easy to tell what someone's thinking. When a catgirl types that her ears are flat and back against her head I know that means she's angry or scared. We drive beneath an overpass and exit near downtown where the road holds nothing but motel after motel. I wonder about the people inside them, their cars parked in front of their rooms, if they're traveling in and out of cities, if they, too, smoke meth and drink in the middle of the night. If any of them are Exxon. If they're older like Mikaela's dad or young like me.

At the motel, Shawn stays close to Mikaela. He grabs for her hand and she holds his finger with one of hers. In our passed notes, she considers me her girlfriend, but that is school world. Maybe in motel world our relationship is different. In motel world she means girlfriend, like, a friend who also happens to be a girl. But it's hard to imagine other friends I would kiss the way she kisses me. Shawn pours drinks, rum into plastic cups of Diet Coke with bagged ice kept in the bathroom sink. I hide my hot cheeks behind my cup. We play an SNES hooked up to the tiny TV and Mason breaks out a bag of cocaine and starts cutting it up on the dresser. He asks if I want some. I don't know, I tell him.

"I would never let you do anything that would hurt you," he says. He's bent over, the heavy bottle of rum next to him, his sharp little teeth in his wide, sappy mouth. When I take a bump Mikaela takes sips from her cup. I rub my face and my eyes suck into the back of my skull. I want to smoke a cigarette so I go outside with Bobby and Shawn to the gritty sizzle of tires on the road. I roll onto the tips of my toes and back to my heels as fireworks pop in the distance.

NUDES

"Sounds like the 'burbs are being shelled," Bobby says. Shawn laughs, then he coughs and spits.

"America's over," Shawn replies. His hair is Cobain blonde and some spit gets stuck to the scrabble of his beard.

"Yeah, fuck this country," I say. Shawn brings his cigarette to his mouth, looks in the direction of the boom-then-crackle of a firework.

I go back into the room and feel his indifference on my skin. The sun sets behind the mountains tinging the sky in orange before bruising inside out. Mikaela dances in front of the bed and I join her, wondering if Shawn or Mason will watch as I dance, if Shawn would become aroused or upset. The Weather Channel is muted, and Shawn puts on house music. I take another bump and imagine my catgirl self dancing for Exxon in her school uniform, a big bell on a collar around her neck. Mason snaps pictures with his camera. Mikaela hooks her finger into the bracelet on my arm, twists it tighter, pulls my wrist up to her face. She licks it, pushes into me, and we fall onto the bed. Shawn pulls out what looks like a whipped cream canister, girthy and silver, and Mikaela puts her hand on my chin. She says, "You're gonna be a porn star one day, I can feel it." Her mouth speaks against my neck, forceful and wet. Mason's camera flashes as Mikaela unbuttons my pants. I sit up and stop her, point to Shawn. "What is that?" I ask.

Shawn puts his mouth on the tap of the whip cream and sucks. A slow, monstrous laugh three octaves too deep leaves his chest. He hands me the canister. I place the plastic tip to my lips, pull the trigger, and breathe in. 'Hooch' by Everything blares on the stereo, and I forget where I am. I lean against Mikaela and lick my wrists, then nuzzle into her neck.

"You make me purr," I say.

"What the fuck," Mikaela laughs. She pushes me away, breathless and manic, and starts jumping up and down on the bed. I jump, too, watching myself in the mirror. I'm just a normal girl with jeans and a thrift store t-shirt, a girl without cat ears or a tail. I want to go home to my computer. My head starts to feel like a deflated balloon and I lose sense of space and time. I feel a cloud of hair against my face, the smell of pink shampoo. I put out my tongue, searching for skin. I can't remember if it's a weekend or a weeknight or if I have to be back at school tomorrow. I'm more afraid of Mikaela's feelings than her touch. It's men that frighten me; their blunt actions like impersonal violence.

Mason does another bump, then holds the key beneath my nostril, cradling my head like I'm a baby. I take the bump, he touches my face, and it's the closest I've ever been to a boy. He shoots another photo of me, my eyes lolling upward, into a painful dark. The room is lit only by the Weather Channel, displaying damaged homes on the beach after a hurricane, like rotting teeth in the mouth of the ocean. I read the scroll of closed captions as fast as I can, but most details are lost.

Shawn looks at the TV and I see the tattoo on his larynx: a woman, classic pinup style, between two nautical stars. She's blonde with blue eyes; her skin is his. Shawn coughs again and the woman's body undulates with his throat. I envision my avatar, the red text of my name burning bright against the computer screen, sending Exxon all the photos: *I know what it means, now.* Mason frames another shot as Shawn sits down on the bed and takes my hand, resting it on Mikaela's stomach. The tattoo girl's legs are spread open, like the wings of an eagle.

NUDES

1

MICHELLE LOOKED LIKE she was hungover. She had some internal fear of missing out. She said if she didn't drink regularly the nightmares would come back, she didn't know how to explain them. If she didn't stay up drinking, she ended up in bed at midnight, listening to her friends play pop music, laughing, smoking cigarettes on the patio. Drinking a few nights a week helped. Then she'd talk to me about it. There was no difference now between drunk Michelle and the other Michelle. "I don't know if I can do it," she said as I drove her to the gas station.

I worked to whittle down to the specifics. "It" could have been her full-time job. "It" could have been our engagement— wedding planning, commitment, etc. "It" could have been sobriety, it could have been anything. I put my hand on her knee. "You can," I said. It was an empty expression, exaggerated by compassion. I hoped she would drop it so I didn't have to spend the next few hours being her therapist.

"Smokes?" she said when we pulled into the lot.

Her lips were wet. Otherwise I might've thought I was kissing a toy. One time she fell asleep with her eyes open and I put my ear next to her mouth, in the off-chance she'd stopped breathing. I wanted her to see how I felt but all she saw was the back of my rain jacket as I walked into the gas station.

"You didn't get the forty," she said. We'd made it back to my friend Wendy's condo; Wendy was at Lake Tahoe with an ex. The rain had stopped. A bit of sun sparkled on the cement walk. Michelle bit her lip so hard it was bleeding. She'd pulled her knees to her chest, placed her chin in the valley of her entwined knuckles.

"Michelle, let's not drink tonight." I knew it wouldn't land. I wanted to feel close to her body without its heaviness slogging deadly on me. Asking her this way had never worked before, but I didn't know what else to say.

"Oh please," she said.

"Naturally," I sighed, kicking the front door open with my foot. Michelle put our bags down and looked around the front room.

"I have to work tomorrow," she said. "And that means I need to sleep tonight."

I couldn't remember the last time I'd fucked her while she was an active participant in her life. Instead, every night when she closed her eyes I locked myself in the bathroom, lay on the bathmat, and thought about Wendy, or the gas station clerk, or Michelle's best friend. It was like a scene from a mumblecore film: we'd meet at a coffee shop or some other middle-class hang out and end up sneaking away to my car or back to their apartment, them taken by lust for me. I'd squeeze around my fingers and climax, unmoored by my misplaced need.

Now Wendy was texting me her list of demands. I'd never fuck her in real life, much less the way I imagined. In my fantasies, I was always the passive one, being taken by her; Wendy wearing a massive strap-on, a pinstripe blazer.

"I want something to drink," Michelle said. "There's no food in the fridge, either."

"I guess I'll fuck off then," I said.

"Can you get some eggs for the hangover?"

"I'll see you in a bit," I said. I shut the condo door behind me, dragged my feet across the low pile carpet in the hallway.

Michelle opened the door just enough. "Two Colt 45s please," she shouted,

"Fuck," I breathed, gripping my phone. "No matter how hard I try."

The rain had picked up again. There wasn't a single dollar store within a five mile radius of Wendy's so I ventured over to my side of town, near the freeway. There was a song on the radio, a poppy sound Michelle would love. The female singer wailed out something about the cyclical nature of avoiding one's feelings, developing bad habits. It was dumb, but I teared up when she sang about throwing up in the bathtub. I imagined Michelle in a similar scenario in the tub: without me, who would help? I stopped for coffee, my plastic bags of eggs, corndogs, potted meat, and individual frozen meals rustling in the passenger seat. I'd picked up the forties, bought a halfpint of Burnett's.

I pulled into Wendy's spot and sat there checking my phone. Strands of hair fell around my face, the smell of Wendy's salon-quality shampoo and conditioner with it. Her perfumed body lotion was on my arms; something Chanel. I used her nail polish, her hair ties, and now I was wearing her teal blue fair isle sweater and her thick, black denim jeans. The jeans cost more money than I could make in a month.

A car pulled in next to me, a neighbour. I imagined myself as Wendy for a moment. My hair was dark like hers, tied up in the same messy bun. I wore minimal make up the way she did—lacking half my eyebrows, but in a chic way. I looked down at my phone and my wrangle of bags and looked back up again. I wondered if the neighbour might mistake me for Wendy, or for an intruder, maybe. Adrenaline rose through the substrate. "I'm Thomas," said the man. Glare on his glasses shielded his eyes. If I followed the curve of his lip with my finger it'd spell M. We walked together to Wendy's condo five stories up and stopped one door down. Why not just do it, I thought, putting my plastic bags down. He stepped inside his apartment, shook his phone at me, said he'd give me a ring.

I dragged the bags into the foyer, careful not to rustle them. I slipped off my tennis shoes and went into the bedroom. Michelle had shut the bathroom door. The bed was plush, like a hotel bed, shades of peachy pink. Above the bed was an oil painting of five nymph-like nudes dancing in an ecstatic circle. The bathroom vent was on, yellow light fanning from the bottom of the door. I leaned into it and cupped my hands to my ear.

"I'm not sure what I'm doing," Michelle said. "No. No wedding. None of that." I heard a drag from a cigarette. A rough blast of breath. "She'll be fine. No. I don't know when I'll tell her."

It was unusual for me and a new feeling. For the past few months we'd talked about marriage, and I admitted to a deep, insolent push inside of me to have children. For most of my life I'd been trained not to want marriage. Or to want children. It came from nowhere—I'd been an only child; had never taken care of anyone younger than me. I'd accidentally killed small pets. Upon graduating high school I told my parents I wanted to be a hair dresser and they said: choose college or Army. I was apathetic at nineteen, starving myself and found no respite in the spiritual or moral guidance of men but through the absolution of my body, the only material icon I could control. My dream body haloed above my highest desires like a porcelain Mary ringed by prismatic quartz.

I lost my balance and walked out towards the wide, green-blue-grey view of the city on the balcony. The air was cool like an open fridge. I missed Wendy. For the last two nights we'd been sleeping in the bed Wendy slept in with her now-estranged husband. It had been four or five days since Michelle and I'd last fucked. It hadn't been easy for us the past few years, or rather, maybe she thought it was easy but she was a difficult person. Perhaps it was my darkest secret. That I wasn't enjoying myself as much as she was, but I didn't know how to work it out, how to make myself happy. I leaned backward over the railing as far as I could, looking up at the other balconies, then to the right, through Thomas's sliding glass doors. He stumbled through the living room out of his shirt and boxers, his face blank like a bag of cereal, and laid upside down onto the plush grey couch with his legs against the backrest and his head toward the floor. He spread his arms out across the couch like the body of Christ.

I didn't think he could see me and I took out my phone to zoom in closer. I wanted to see his expression more clearly and snapped a few pixelated photos. His hand slowly brushed across his crotch, the tip disappearing then reappearing between his forefinger and thumb. The stroking was delicate at first then Thomas got more vigorous. He straightened his legs out and swept them over his body, bending his back so far his toes came right to the hardwood floor. His ass looked like two beautiful hills. Through my phone screen the figure of Thomas pressed the tip of his cock to his mouth, licking at it first, then pushing the lower half of his body with his hands to take it all. From Wendy's apartment, the bathroom door swung open and I snapped my last picture, almost dropping my phone. On the couch I rubbed the blood out of my cheeks as Michelle walked in. I turned my engagement ring over and over on my finger and started in on my pint. My hands shook as I poured a shot then took a chaser. I couldn't get my mind off Thomas's delicate tongue, the shape of his cock. Most striking to me was the sybaritic look in his eyes, his eyelids tender and half-closed. I went into the bathroom and texted Wendy and turned the vent on. She was the only person I trusted with everything, the first woman I had sex with. We'd been friends since seventh grade.

"I need to talk to you," I texted. I sent a quick paragraph of what was going on. Five minutes later she called. "So, she's still drinking," Wendy said. "Tell me how you're feeling about all of this?"

Wendy's voice was unanimously comforting. It may have been the vodka but I let loose: I'm not even using my college degree, I whined. Everything is customer service, I'm too nice, I love Michelle, deeply, but we don't want the same things and it makes me hurt in some intangible way. Wendy gave me all the room I needed to process and always gave the most accurate advice. And, after all of that, I said, And your neighbour?

"Yeah?"

Do you know him, I asked.

"Yeah," she said. "He seems nice."

The next morning, Michelle woke up refreshed and commuted to work in my car while I called in sick. I rummaged through Wendy's medicine cabinet and found tabs of Xanax and took a pill. I turned on the TV and watched a rerun of *Grace Under Fire*. I marveled at how well Brett Butler's style, inspired by '90s grunge, and her braided bleached hair looked stylish today, as though everything had come full circle. I settled back on the couch, letting the medication wash over my body. I wondered what Thomas was doing. I decided I needed to wake up and feel productive, so I slipped out of my pyjamas. Wendy had recently renovated the bathroom. The shower head was an enormous square with water that fell from it like rain dripping. I grabbed Michelle's electric toothbrush and brought it into the shower with me. The colour of Thomas's tongue on his cock had stayed with me. Everything in his apartment was the same pale cream colour of his skin, except for the shock of pink in his lips and mouth. I placed the back of the buzzing toothbrush to me, imagining myself in Thomas's apartment. He lay on a lush bed with white sheets, shirt draped across his body like a hellenic robe. I leaned in for a kiss, instead the film disintegrated, and I saw Michelle, the crêpey-creasing of her eyes when she's below me, about to come. I felt a sudden stab of loss, and again moved to something else—Wendy at sixteen, her ass flat against the bed, strawberry lube and Pocari Sweat on my breath. It was getting me there. My hands sloshed against the water collecting around my arms. My phone pinged. I opened my eyes, the glare of yellow light against the glass shower door. The water was running cold, and my fingers were tight and pruny.

I got out of the shower and I checked my phone. "She returns to beauty," from Thomas. "What do you do for fun?" I told him I liked to paint. My favourite paintings were of bodies stretched thin and bony with fat deposits in the normal places. "Eerie," he said, then he sent me an iMDB page to a short film. I searched and found the film online. The camera zoomed out from a body sealed between two sheets of clear plastic, pressed with flowers and foliage between the body's legs. From far away it looked like a mannequin. Another scene showed the same beige body, seconds before being shrink-wrapped. The legs looked hairy, or it could have been sprigs of dill. The plastic around the body sucked shut, smoothing out her skin, the body embossed with flora. A hole had been cut for the mouth, where her red lips sucked like a sphincter.

"Restricted bodies, like your paintings," Thomas texted.

"You've never seen them," I replied.

"I can google, too," he said. I sat down on the bed and loosely wrapped one of Wendy's soft towels around me. "Each time I restart the video, it's still exciting," he said. "It's like I forget the thrill of the vacuum turning on and watching that plastic seal shut."

I imagined the drone camera panning out from Wendy's window, a view of my pockmarked back open to the city. Thomas on his gray couch staring, also, at his phone. We were of anatomical symmetry in the same body."

Some people will do anything to be taken care of," I replied.

Michelle came home and I spent most of dinner quiet, thinking about how Thomas and I would never touch. If it would be better that way—never touching, but only studying each other Something perfect and dopamine-soaked and contained. I had wanted it this way, contained, as we'd walked up the stairs and to the elevator then through the hallway. I told him about the housesitting. I wasn't rich, I admitted, and his curiosity about me continued. He was curious about slumming, it seemed, and I wondered if I would be that slum. Michelle drank, and slept, and left for work, and I asked Thomas what he did with his days.

"I've ghost written TV scripts," he said. "There's only one thing I want to perfect and that is the logos, the pure sound of language." I asked if he could complete that with something like a TV script.

"For now I'm just interested in making pretty girls talk," he said.

Wendy came back. The rest of the week I spent at home, deleting my back and forth messages with Thomas. He sent me art films and I imagined the nudity within as his nudity, then looked at the pictures of him on my phone. I understood myself as a series of words generically rearranging themselves into a TV script. Friday night I put my phone away. Michelle wanted to stay up late, acetone on her breath.

"I miss you," she said. The sound of my voice repeating her words was wide and open in the room but when her body came closer to mine, I made a little *oh* sound. It was too close, like I was getting to know myself and didn't like it. When she was away from me, her body sitting up like that, I could forget she was there. Be less nervous about her presence, over-thinking every moment. I brushed my fingers around the insignificant dots on her nipples. I painted scenes, vivid brush strokes of oil paintings, one lanky, long and ribby body bending over another in a C, the other with large breasts and a thin waist with smooth expensive skin. I realised after a few moments I'd been too quiet, and came to with the sound of smacking skin. Each thrust hit harder until I felt myself give. It wasn't ecstatic, but uncomfortable, and yet something in me wanted to continue. Pleasing Michelle was the only thing that mattered.

NUDES

Michelle licked a finger and touched the cold tip to me, lighting alive like the cherry of a cigarette. That's my girl, she said. She leaned down to kiss and parted her mouth, like a goat reaching for grass, gripping my lips with a heady, engulfing press.

I looked around our room. Its junk made it austere: heavy mahogany nightstands, a dresser with gold handles. Nothing matched. Michelle got up to go the bathroom and I leaned over the bed to check my phone.

"In school they tell you to say why you like something," a message said. "I didn't like school, though." When I imagined Thomas's face I thought of myself becoming a pure, endless data signal. Michelle came back with a wet hand towel and cleaned herself. "Being in love with you exhausts me," she said. "Sex sobers me up too much." She yawned and lay next to me on the mattress.

I picked up the remote and suggested a movie.

"Oh, sure," Michelle said. She left the room and came back with a glass of vodka. I scrolled through the TV guide slowly, reading each description with squinted eyes. I stopped on a film set in the late 1980s about a bruisy, decades-long romance that didn't last.

Later, I walked nude to the kitchen, phone as flashlight, to get Michelle another drink. For a long time I stood there staring at my phone, letting the cool air bring bumps to my skin. I'd sent Thomas pictures of my paintings, nudes; interpretations of the body I wished I could have. Fake breasts, plump cheeks, horrific veneers. Markers of status. A populist beauty that was egalitarian because it could be bought; to mutilate in the name of self-love. Loving grotesque. I wanted to be like that, beautiful and horrible. Thomas seemed to know this. Everything was now filtered through the painting of us; I wanted it to feel like Goya, and Thomas in my mind was painting Goya.

"What is it you want?" another text. "You should get what you want." My pulse thudded towards a determined end. I'd see him run a hand through his dark hair, or his eyelids skimming a surface of want. I'd made up scenes in my head: streaky oil strokes of us in a red plastic booth eating cheap croissants, bloodshot and black in chiaroscuro highlight. We moved like bad animation. I flipped again through the still shots I had of him on my phone. His pursuit of himself felt personal, not contrived of convention or the expectations of others. I had tried to sketch it by pen and covered it in lies. Our experience together would only be paint.

2

Mistaken. Michelle always looked that way. She hated men in particular, but quoted Camille Paglia once: "If civilisation had been left in female hands, we would still be living in grass huts." In school, bullies hurt her. In college, her parents cut Michelle off. She had transformed, she said, into the purest version of herself. The nightmares were just leftovers.

She tipped her glass toward Wendy, clinked it, pulled her lips back to smile in that way she does when she's working to make other people believe she's relatable. Other guests in the room clamoured on, congregating on Wendy's white leather couch. Thomas stood next to the sliding glass door curling liquor around in a glass and I stared past him, out the balcony, into the black skyline blurred by rain. He'd cut his hair, shorn close to the scalp, and had a little grit on his jaw.

"It's a fucking icebox in here, right?" Michelle said, and I removed my cardigan for her; rubbed my arms. I kept my eyes at the melting city. Everyone else was sporting a faux tan. Thomas turned his head. He noticed my clavicles first. An impulse of him biting them crossed my mind. I was wearing too much eyeliner and a black choker.

"This is weird ... I don't know any of the people here," Michelle said. "I thought Wendy said it would be a casual thing, but this is like networking. Drink four, down the hatch. Want another?"

"I guess."

Michelle put her chin in my shoulder. "Lighten up," she said. She looked sober enough to still make rational decisions, for whatever reason.

"Make me another," I said. "And make another one for yourself."

"Yes ma'am." She pretended to salute me and walked back to the card table, picked at cheese. I went into the living room under the pretense of looking for Wendy. I kept my gaze on the sliding glass door, slid it open, and walked onto the balcony. I lit a cigarette, wishing I'd had my cardigan. Little drops of rain spit on my face as I leaned over the railing. I felt death there. Then I felt the heat of Thomas's body. I ashed my cigarette and turned to look.

"I'm Thomas," he said, putting out a hand. "I wanted to make it look official." He nodded toward the living room, picked up my soft pack, and spanked a cigarette out of it.

"Don't squish it," I said.

"I won't." He put the pack back on the table and lit the cigarette. Inside, other bodies talked to each other. Michelle was talking to Wendy, moving her hands around.

"I didn't know you were with someone," he said. "You've been eye fucking me all night."

"I'm *not*."

"Not now."

I reached over to pick up my glass; I smelled hints of his cologne, geranium and cedar. He took the drink out of my hand and wetness seeping to the corners of his mouth as he took a sip. I heard my name called from inside, and put my arms around myself, my skin numb and dulled.

Wendy pulled me into a group of women, nodding enthusiastic-
ally at another person. "I know. Yeah. Yeah. That's what Maxine
said … mhmm …" She squeezed my shoulders hard and turned
her mouth to my ear. "Am I seeing things, or are you making
a new friend?"

I whispered back. "Sure—but it's not—not what it looks
like." A girl from the group squealed, "It's not a clit piercing—
it's just the hood!"

Wendy rolled her eyes, and turned her head towards the
kitchen, nodded accusingly. Michelle took a deep drink, leaned
forward and laughed with a woman, then pushed a strand of the
woman's hair behind her ear.

"You're not the only one," Wendy whispered.

"I heard her tell someone in the bathroom last week"—A
peal of laughter from the group—"I heard her talking to someone," I said. I felt the wall giving.

"And?" Wendy mouthed.

"I think she's gonna call off the engagement."

Wendy looked at my hands as I absent-mindedly turned the
stone around on my ring finger. A cigarette butt streaked red
over the balcony from the corner of my eye. "Fucked up,"
Wendy said, "but unlikely. You're worrying too much."

I swallowed, gave a nod.

"Why don't I try talking to her?" She squeezed the top of
my arm again.

The group had broken off. I slid away and went to make
myself another drink. I'd been counting Michelle's, but lost track
and decided it didn't matter. I poured vodka and looked off into
Wendy's bedroom, lost in the rectangle of light, the corner of her
quilt, and the nymphic nudes above the headboard. Normally

it didn't bother me but I felt overwhelmed with everything I didn't have, as though I could have had a better life if I'd made different decisions. I wondered if Michelle was part of that. I zigzagged through the crowd towards the bedroom's bathroom and closed the door. I let my ass meet the counter, sipping in the dark. I wanted to grieve alone like a dying animal. My mind moved to painting, and I traced the curve of Thomas's iliac crest with my free hand in the dark, imagined my hand caressing the tight flesh of his thigh, pulling out the stroke until the leg was twice the length of his torso, bent painfully at the knee. Next, his arm reaching just as far towards my neck, the elbow exaggerated like a knot in a rope, wringing me loose. Then the door opened, an armed reached in and flipped on the light.

"Oh, sorry," Thomas said. "I thought it was empty. Are you sitting here alone in the dark?" The light caught his cheekbones showcasing a few acne scars. I looked up and pursed my mouth, my face warping into something pitiable.

"Christ," he said. "What's going on with you?" His tone was overfamiliar, it felt foreign to be talking to him so up close and personal.

"I looked you up online, you know."

He shifted his weight. The bathroom's brown, stone-tiled walls encased me, and I made mental notes to remember the comfort of it, wanting to replicate the look in my fantasy house with my fantasy wife.

"I thought the famous last name was just a coincidence."

Thomas looked at his phone and unlocked the home screen. "She makes you mad, doesn't she."

"You're avoiding the question," I said.

"You didn't ask me a question." His glasses slid down his nose.

"Yes, she makes me so mad," I conceded. I imagined throwing Michelle through the glass doors, over the balcony, my ring in her palm. Though I couldn't arrange so artful an ending. I had no thrust for drama. "The thing is she will never think her behaviour is wrong. She maintains it's a perceptual issue on my part."

"From what you've said, it sounds isolating." It was, I said.

Thomas hooked an arm around my neck, pulling me out of the bathroom. The party'd gotten louder—drinks sloshing, music and dimmed the lights, a girl smoking on the couch. I panned the room for Wendy or Michelle. Thomas pulled me towards the front door. I lit a cigarette as soon as we were out on the street.

"I finally get it," Thomas said. I handed him the smoke and he took a drag.

"Where are you taking me?" I felt alive with difference— nighttime in a new neighbourhood, a transubstantiated kind of life. Cars buzzed by and Thomas raised his arms, his shirt ruffling in the wind.

"You make fake nudes of yourself to sell as art so you don't have to reveal yourself to anyone in actuality."

"Is that your deep, philosophical analysis of me?"

"It's your animal brain."

The wind whipped his hair back, making his face look long.

"Do you tell all women you spend time with that they lack a frontal cortex?"

"Just you," he said. "You'd be happier without."

A half mile up the street was a bar that advertised pinball and arcade games. The bar booth was boldcoloured, sticky and childlike, and Thomas brought back manhattan after manhattan. We sucked the cherries out of the empty glasses. Then after that is a bit of a blur. At some point I reached over the table and took off his glasses, saw his features growing older. Fantasies had become completely replaced by new ones—something stolid, stable and bright with green grass.

"You really do look like your father," I remember saying.

"Banal," Thomas said. "It's the chin."

We got back to the condo and Thomas locked the door, took off his coat. It was a mirror image of Wendy's. I waited for Thomas to make his intentions known, for what was coming next. It was dark in the room, but all the expensive objects refracted light, these daydreamy things pointed at me. I was afraid that once I broke a boundary I couldn't repair it. But Thomas looked bored. I felt small inside myself. Stupid, stupid, stupid, I muttered. We were already this. I separated parts of myself into categories: smart self, sexy self, sad self, manipulative self. I didn't know which one to be. Again, another fragment. After this Thomas was over me, shoulders shrink-wrapped in sweat. His glasses fogged so I couldn't see his eyes, but I liked it because it felt less personal. His body eclipsed light from the balcony and the M in his lips pulled back in a sneer, showing teeth. I sucked breath in quick to let him know I felt good, or felt something, that this thing happening between us was interesting, but I don't think he was even hard. We kissed once and the sweetness of mixer had coated my mouth. I couldn't be sure anything had happened, because I'd woken up alone. The room smelled like cat food.

I got up, looking for my cell phone to check the time and found a few photos from Thomas. At first, I struggled to see. Pieces of the images blew apart then came back together, bit by bit: the familiar silk wallpaper, the velvet and wood Victorian headboard and creamy bed linens. There was the sharp recognition of myself like bumping into a long lost enemy on the street. Every image I took I manipulated before pushing it out into the public sphere. The girl in the nudes was a stranger to me, eyes soft and relaxed, staring warmly into the distance. The length of my body felt shocking. More pieces collected; Thomas's comforting, disparate voice telling me how to position my feet, the vulnerability of moving air as I spread open my legs. I was sad Thomas wasn't here. I wanted to see what my sadness looked like on him. The first picture, again: me in the centre of the headboard. One knee bent to reveal both crescents of my ass. I'd stretched my arms out on either side for balance, the carved and tufted headboard flaring from either side of my shoulders. I looked regal.

GRACE

AT FIRST, THE SPIDERS CAME SLOWLY. I spotted a huge one crawling on the ceiling over the doorway, and I was too afraid to move underneath her. Instead, I watched her—the size of my thumb—crawl onto a wall and behind a hanging frame. Inside the frame is a replica of Dali's *Geopoliticus Child Watching the Birth of the New Man*, the one where the woman and child appear first and they watch as the man struggles to emerge from a tiny eggshaped earth.

I grabbed a can of hairspray and sprayed it at her in hopes she would suffocate. She fell somewhere, possibly behind the TV or bookcase. I wasn't sure if she died, but I left it at that.

It was the middle of the day. My wife was at work. I had quit my job, and so our lives became organised as such: I did domestic chores, she worked. I felt guilty about the arrangement. I had worked since I was a teenager, all through my first marriage, until my late thirties. I was not used to relying on someone else.

Later in the day, I saw another spider. Or the same spider. It was hard to say which. My wife was home, sitting on the couch, enjoying a drink. This time, the spider was on the other side of the room, crawling behind a mirror. I yelled for my wife, because the hairspray didn't work and I had nothing else to protect myself. My wife took her time getting off the couch. I kept my eyes on the spider, and the mirror, the painting by Dali reflected in it—the tiny man being birthed from the earth egg, or being swallowed by it.

"Cup her and take her outside," she said. Before she could even finish, I'd grabbed a shoe and smashed the thing against the wall. When I removed the shoe, it left behind a wet, oily mark and a single despondent leg. I didn't look under the shoe.

I felt sort of bad, but pushed it out of my memory, thinking that now I could sleep at night without worrying about the spider.

The next day, my wife called me from work.

"Don't forget to water the plants," she said. I walked into the kitchen to fill the watering can. On the linoleum, a tiny spider, similar in shape and colour to the one I'd killed, crawled to the middle of the floor. I stepped over her to grab the broom from the pantry. When I turned around, she was gone. I bent down on my hands and knees to look for the spider, but did not see her anywhere. When I got up from the floor, I'd already forgotten why I'd gone into the kitchen.

The bromeliad was dying. Our apartment doesn't get much natural sun, and the tiny rosebushes I'd been gifted earlier in the year had died within two weeks. I put the bromeliad on a desk near an east-facing window. I poured water over the centre cup of leaves, where the large, bright-pink stamen with its white and purple buds protruded about one foot up. Four thick layers of green, aloe-like leaves sprayed out from this stamen and formed the cup into which I poured water.

It had been close to a month since my wife had brought it home. The tag from the store was still on it, because I often forgot how to take care of things.

That evening, my wife and I were sitting on the couch watching some form of American TV, the kind where you pay for the luxury of avoiding commercials. A tiny shadow moved across the wall, and without thinking, I pointed at it, yelling. It reminded me of how I felt programmed to point and scream around my ex-husband, as if my cries were a warning system. Like the time we were barreling down Exeter Street at 45 miles per hour, and a car suddenly pulled in front of us to turn left. Had I not screamed and pointed, we would have collided. It was like some force inside of me took over, possessed my body, flew into my mouth, right through to the tips of my fingers and pointed, screaming to keep us alive.

"Will you get a cup?" I asked. She was lying on me, so I figured she would be the first to get up.

"Yes," she said. But she lay there, still watching the TV. Without commercial breaks, it was always demanding someone's attention. The shadowy spot on the wall continued to move, bobbing along the uneven bumps of paint as if they were rolling foothills. In fear of losing this battle, I got up instead. My wife adjusted herself—upset, perhaps, that I'd disturbed her comfort. I grabbed a cup from the kitchen and a piece of junk mail from the dining room table. When I cupped the spider, the creature seemed to get upset as well, maybe for the same reasons as my wife. I slid the thin piece of mail between the cup and the wall, and tipped the cup right side up. Her legs were thin, twice as long as her body, and dotted white and brown. She was not very large, perhaps the size of my fingernail in length. Still, the odd shape of her body, and how disproportionate her legs were to my own body, spurred a deep restlessness in my chest that made me dislike her presence.

"What kind of spider do you think it is?" I asked. "I'm not sure," my wife replied. "A brown recluse, maybe?"

I took pictures of the spider with my phone.

"It could be a wolf spider," she said. "Recluses are the ones that stay hidden. Wolf spiders like to hunt, so likely they're the ones crawling everywhere."

I took the cup out to the patio, removed the junk mail lid, and flung the cup so that she went flying, far away from the apartment. Again, I pushed the incident out of my memory, so I could sleep at night.

The bromeliad continued to die, no matter how much sun it received or how much water I gave it. The entire bottom layer of once thick leaves shriveled into black, rotten ones that splayed out from the plant like discarded banana skins. It was not a good look. I thought back to the almost-accident with my ex-husband. We had been discussing his drinking and our money situation. The air outside had been cold, and in the warmth of the car I could smell his unbrushed teeth. His mouth had the distinct smell of old, sweet corn. Money was tight, but I had been pushing him to save for a house. I had been wanting something bigger—to have my own space, farther away from the noise that seemed inseparable from his presence. Most of our extra money—several hundred dollars per month—was going to alcohol. The near-death from our almost-collision halted the conversation, and I was only reminded of it when he was drunk and we were lying in bed together. He would be asleep, lulled by the booze, and I would be awake, thinking of his habit and how I could not control it.

One night, the dog whined at our door, scratching to be let out. It was loud enough that my ex-husband woke up.

"Did you feed the dog?" he asked. His food bowl had been empty since the night prior, and so had his bowl of water.

"I'm sorry," I replied. "I always forget."

He had come back from the bathroom and squatted near the bed to plug in his phone. He was nude. I could see a droplet of piss glistening on the tip of his penis, and wondered how often and how much of his body fluids were left on the sheets. His body, when he was drunk, was always slightly damp from sweat, and the smell of it was of old skin, dirty from working. The stale residue of cigarette smoke was on his breath, beads of cold fluid in his hair.

"What do you think would have happened if I hadn't screamed?" I asked.

"Probably nothing," he said. "I saw the car turning. I would have stopped." I wanted to think that I had changed the course of our lives somehow, and was indignant when he would not acknowledge this.

"You don't think your reaction time would have been different?" I asked.

"No. I don't believe that I have any say in when I die or don't die."

"Don't you feel like everyone else thinks that, and that's why they are scared of death?"

"There are no choices I can make that guarantee I won't die tomorrow," he said.

He got back into bed. During the first part of our marriage, I enjoyed the ways our skin met when he moved his body against mine. Eventually, though, his body spilled too far into my space.

If his face was turned toward me and he was snoring slightly or breathing too heavily, I found myself annoyed at his presence. A glistening drop of water looked delicious and pure on a glass of whiskey, but less appealing on his skin. It was the context surrounding the water that determined its purity, its desirability.

The dog ate quietly in the kitchen.

"You have to get better at feeding the dog," he added. "And ask yourself why you don't make it a priority. Ignoring the problem is immoral."

My body began to itch, as if the unease I felt about the wolf spider was somehow moving from the inside of my body to the outside. I dismissed it as my being too sensitive, given that I was now seeing a spider at least once a day. The morning after I threw the tiny one out, I went for a walk and picked flowers for my hair. I thought of the times I would walk the dog when I was still with my ex-husband, who had taken custody of him in our divorce. I left the flowers in a cup on the dining room table and went to make myself lunch. I sat down at the table to eat. Another little shadow, similar to the one I saw on the wall, moved toward me, away from the cup, which was the only place I could picture it having come from.

"Uhh," I said.

"Uhh," was a sound of indecisiveness. It was as though my brain had short-circuited. A memory of the dog blipped in my mind. I remembered how I had been the one to push my ex-husband to get him, and had told him I'd be the one responsible. But when we did get him, I would beg my ex-husband to walk him when the dog woke up before sunrise, scratching to go out. I got up and grabbed another cup and another piece of junk mail. When I cupped the spider, I worried that I'd killed her, because as soon as I slipped the mail underneath the cup, she stopped moving. I flipped the cup over, and the spider crawled up the edges, trying to escape, so I knew then at least she was not dead.

I removed the spider from the house, but the itchiness continued. A few hairs on my head would move, as though something was crawling on me. I sat with my feet underneath the desk, and the itchy feeling was on my toes, or in places I could not see. Sometimes it would be in my ears, or on the back of my neck. The next day, I was moving the scale, which was set up against the bathroom wall, so I could weigh myself. On the other side was another spider. I dropped the scale and she scurried underneath the bathroom counter. This time, I did not go looking for a cup, or for her.

By now, the bromeliad was completely dead despite the watering. The leaves were a mix of pale sulfur-yellow and black, and the stamen was desiccated to the touch. Although it looked dead, it was still somehow beautiful, so I did not throw it out. I knew my wife would be upset that I'd killed the plant, so I hid it in the pantry, a place she would not look often.

In the kitchen, I saw another spider crawl toward the fridge. I remembered what my wife said about them, how they hunt. I wasn't sure what spiders ate, but I opened the fridge and placed a morsel of something meaty on the floor. She seemed suspicious at first, but then crawled onto it. I turned around to fill up the watering can for the bromeliad, and when I looked back, both the morsel and the spider were gone.

The next day, there were two spiders in the kitchen, waiting by the fridge. I pulled more pieces of meat out to feed them. They again seemed unsure of my offering. But I walked away, and when I returned, both the food and the spiders were gone. I began to respect the relationship we were building, in the hopes that they would leave me alone. But at the same time, the unusual shapes of their bodies left me in unease. With all of the spiders I was seeing, I was unable to sleep at night. I was having visions of my ex-husband and car accidents, of times I'd disappointed him with my minuscule failings; of disembodied insect legs, their wet amputated ends, crawling all over my skin and in my hair. After any sleep I did get, I would wake up, still feeling itchy all over. I began to shower every morning, to shave my legs and my arms, but the itchy feeling kept coming back. It was as though the hairs growing out of me were the same disembodied legs, crawling all over my skin. I shaved my eyebrows, and then my face, and eventually my whole body, including my head. I repeated this ritual every morning, to the dismay of my wife. Afterward, I stepped out of the shower to stare at myself in the mirror. There was something slightly unsettling about my hairless appearance, which I liked. I stared at my body from different angles, admiring how round and new my head looked, how simple my face appeared without eyebrows. I ran my hands down the length of my arms, removing droplets of water, approving of how easily my fingers slipped across the smooth surface of my skin. Perhaps I was seeing myself more objectively. I would be free of the itchy feeling for a few hours, but then the itchiness would return.

Over the next few days, three and then four spiders would show up. They grew from the size of my fingernail to the size of my thumb. They came in larger and larger groups, and what was once novelty turned into duty.

When I looked at them, I waited for some desire to be born in me, but nothing came. By this point, I was also no longer able to sleep. Along with the car accidents, I dreamt of dozens of spiders among the sheets, waiting for and wanting food. I stayed awake, obsessing over my morning shower, over each stroke of the razor across my skin to get the itching to stop. When I finally fell into a deep sleep, I dreamt about dragging the razor across my skull, about how satisfying it felt removing one long strip of hair and the top layer of skin with it. I continued to drag the razor along the same strip, over and over again, until a hole was formed. The contents of my skull spilled out of it like a wet egg, and from the contents emerged a homunculus of my ex-husband. I woke up that morning and decided to cook a feast, hoping that it would be the end of the spiders' begging.

I prepared a large meal of roasted pork, which I had rubbed and marinated. I cut large pieces of zucchini in half and placed them in a pan to grill. I had my wife bring home a loaf of French bread, as this would be a special occasion. She obliged me, something my ex would not have done. It was late in the afternoon, and the itchiness had already returned to my body, heavy with exhaustion. I was scratching my arms, my legs and the top of my head as I cooked the meal. I felt pleased with my ability to multitask. I set the table, and placed the dead brome-liad in the centre. My wife seemed distrustful, and surprised at the return of the dead plant that had, in her mind, been gone for months. I sat at the head of the table, freshly razored, and our delicious feast sat in the middle. My wife bent her head, as if ready to say some sort of grace. We had never said grace before, but the same sense of guttural force, of the almost-accident, overtook me in the moment—as if somehow, saying some kind of grace, any grace, was needed. I looked over to the extra plate I'd set, just one, for the many spiders we would feed.

DEAD TO ME

WE BOUGHT A CAR. We bought a house. We bought a dog. A year later, we had a baby. Health insurance covered half the hospital bills. We paid the rest with a credit card, maxed out at twenty-one percent APR. The hospital charged forty dollars to place the baby on my chest.

The baby turned eight months old. He cried every night, after dinner until bed. It happened when I turned the faucet on to shower. It overwhelmed me every time. This time when the baby wailed, I waited for Logan's voice from the living room. Instead, I heard only infantile sobbing.

I raced into the living room, soaked in a towel, and kicked a wooden toy with my toe.

Logan sat on the couch playing a video game, something with wizards. Our boy, Ian, lay amidst his scattered toys. I pulled the towel up higher.

Logan watched wizards on the screen throw glowing balls, grunting. His eyes darted between the neon figures.

"Are you going to do anything?"

"No, I'm just going to sit here and let him scream," he said.

NUDES

I walked back into the bathroom and tried to ignore my guilt, but it clung. Water dropped from the ends of my hair. I pumped lotion into my hands and massaged it into my skin. I'd gotten some rash on my hands and hadn't worn my wedding ring in months. My fingers acclimated to life without them, but every morning I woke up and reminded myself I should wear them around my husband.

The baby's screams grew louder, more urgent, and I left the bathroom. My son looked like a radish, howling so hard his body hiccuped for air. He saw me and reached out his arms. When I lay in bed that night, I realised I'd left my rings on the counter again.

Three months into our marriage, Logan told me he felt suicidal. There was nothing wrong with Logan. He had never been to war. He had seen nothing terrible in his life, had killed nothing or no one, not even on accident. No guilt hung over his head at night keeping him awake.

No nightmares terrorised him. He seemed to be a clean, white slate. But in him was an untouchable well of sadness, which made him distant and angry. The more I dug, the deeper the well became. I spent weeks on the internet researching how marriages end, the ones that last less than a year. I thought I had made a mistake, one that was perhaps inescapable.

I held his hand in the dark and said it would be okay. Something else regarding the first night he confessed his inclination to die: I felt suicidal, too. So in our sadness we made a pact. To stay alive, to hang together, the way we vowed on our wedding day.

In our dispute about our son, he'd left the room. I thought, what if this is it? What if this time he kills himself and leaves me alone?

The morning after, I put the kettle on, swept and did the dishes while I waited for the water to boil. I put a load of laundry in the machine, took clean clothes out of the dryer. My days rolled out in a series of KonMari squares, forever folded and tucked into neat, repeating lines.

Logan finished his shower and walked into the kitchen, his hair wet and slicked back. He said nothing of our fight.

"Maybe we should go to therapy," I said, but he shook his head.

"They can't help us," he said. "We suffer from psychological disturbances because our lives are unnatural." I handed him his lunch and gave him a chaste kiss on the cheek. I considered the implications of its chasteness. I imagined the young women in his office—women like I used to be. His shoulders slumped forward, as he crossed the lawn to the car.

The baby slept in his bed, breathy noises coming from the baby monitor. Every day the baby strewed coloured pencils over the living room; crackers crumbed into the couch cracks; yogurt splotched on a newly mopped floor. On their own the offenses were minuscule, but together they loomed large and endless.

Standing at the sink, my vision softened. The fight from the day before entered my vision, and the one before that, and all the days in which my resentment of Logan grew. I imagined my suffering coming out of me like Play-Doh through a push-mold, delicate and exact and pleasant to look at. I imagined alternative universes; one in which Logan died, one in which I died, one in which I had the neighbour's life, one in which we'd never met. A million viable paths, all leading to suffering. If I had taken another path, I'd probably suffer from wanting the things I now had. Back in grad school, I'd taken a yoga class and one regular had gotten pregnant. My envy gripped me. She nannied and her husband was an electrical engineer and in a band. They moved from Portland and had a close family. I was burnt out by my research and fantasised being around children all day while my husband worked. Now I had it. My breasts hurt, I hadn't showered in six days and I had forgotten how to dress myself.

A distant piercing cry broke my spell, and the distance closed between me and the sound, and I found myself sitting at a dining room table where my son curled up in his chair, oatmeal smeared across his chin. I picked up a plastic spoon with soft edges. His hands waved up and down, banged on his chair. I stared at my cell phone, desperate for someone to speak with. I had not spoken with my friends in some time. I had learned not to trust other women's opinions with my marriage, as they seemed ready to validate my feelings, making it hard to discern what was real and what was not.

I thought about calling my mother, but decided against it. My mother avoided talk about emotions, never even said "you're welcome" when she was thanked. Lately, she neglected to ask how I was doing; it was always, "How's the baby? Got any pics?"

In grad school, I concerned myself with the expected worries of a woman approaching her thirties: *Can I make money, can I have a career, how do I find fulfillment, am I going to have a baby*.

What I hadn't considered was life after a baby.

What I hadn't considered was how it reminded me of my mother. The way I mothered: impatient and detached.

I turned on the TV while the baby fished for oatmeal in his bowl. I couldn't stop thinking of my argument with Logan. My level of anger didn't seem justified, but it pulsed anyway, like a plate sliding between my skull and skin. I wanted to live inside a TV commercial. How clean the narrator's voice sounded. No emotional baggage, just the perfect sell.

My phone vibrated; it was Logan. I hoped to hear an apology. Instead, he said he'd be home from work late. Then a peal of laughter echoed in the background.

"You continue to lie," I said. "You continue to lie to me, and I just ask you to tell me the truth and it's fine. It's gone on a long time."

"You're mad," Logan said. "You're always mad for reasons I don't understand."

The baby shrieked and dropped his spoon. I bent down to get it.

"You come home from work and it's like you're off duty," I said. The baby dropped his spoon again and screamed. He tossed his bowl onto the floor with a clatter. I turned away from him.

"We could switch places," said Logan.

"You don't trust me," I cried.

I hung up the phone.

A few days passed, and I forgot the fight. I had taken up stalking my ex online. He was a road comic based in Arizona; he drove back and forth between the midand southwest for gigs. In my darkest moments, I fantasised about the life we could be having.

It'd been years since I'd seen him. One second I stood at the kitchen counter slicing watermelon and in another I scrolled through pictures of him doing stand-up, remembering the time he'd gently popped half a dozen heart-shaped anal beads out my asshole, one by one.

NUDES

I knew he had a girlfriend; they were engaged. He made jokes about dating fat women, but that was for the stage, I thought. When I found her online, I discovered it wasn't just for laughs. She had a blog, a photo-stream, and some small one-off sites with little updates about the upcoming wedding.

I scrolled through dozens of pictures of thin, bronzed women—she worked in fashion photography—until I came upon a few selfies. She had a symmetrical face but was at least a hundred and fifty pounds heavier than I was. She had better skin than I did, too. She'd dyed her hair a vibrant, cotton-candy blue. Worst of all, she looked happy.

Every evening when Logan arrived home, I got into the habit of tossing a frozen meal in the microwave and sat on the couch, ignoring Ian's cries, staring into my phone at her photos. I searched for hashtags—his name, hers, their names combined as if they were a celebrity couple. I found out she had a younger sister who favoured platform shoes and baggy, high-waisted jeans, sharp-angled sunglasses, and bobbed mousy hair. A few photos surfaced of the girlfriend and the comedian with her family over holidays. Dressed in suits and churchy dresses, standing in front of a piano in the lobby of some expensive-looking hotel. Another couple with the comedian's father in the hometown he and I shared. In one of the girlfriend's posts she wrote that their wedding was on the same day as Hitler's birthday.

The relationship with the comedian wasn't better. It was just different. A memory I could project onto, a time when someone obsessed over me because of who I was rather than the things I could do for him.

70

A couple months ago, Mandy and her husband Chaz invited us over for dinner. The weather turned humid and Logan and I brought cans of beer in a cooler we kept in the garage. We maintained a slight buzz for the entire day beforehand, drinking in the sun.

Both families paid for a babysitter and we walked the children up to her house. When we got back, Mandy and Chaz prepared a dinner of roast beef, potatoes, carrots and salad. It was very American. We sat down at the kitchen table in their small house. Mandy sipped white wine from a stemless glass and I spotted a small bottle of Goldschläger on top of the fridge.

We drank beers while I eyed the Goldschläger. Mandy filled our plates with second helpings of beef and potatoes and gravy. The salad sat untouched. Logan and Chaz discussed their jobs, and Chaz announced that he'd gotten fired from his last one. He fidgeted in his chair and didn't say much, and I noticed he drank mineral water, not beer. Mandy wore her uniform from Family Dollar. The name tag pinned to her shirt said *manager*.

I complimented the dinner they'd made for us, and Mandy's mouth split into a smile.

"It's just the crock pot. It does all the work."

We continued to drink, except for Chaz. He got up and put a hand on the back of Mandy's head, stroking his fingers through her dark, curly hair. Chaz said he had to go to the unemployment office early in the morning. When he left for bed, Logan stepped outside to smoke a cigarette. I sat in the kitchen while Mandy cleared plates. I heard the faucet turn on.

She must have seen me eye the bottle on the fridge because she came back with the Goldshläger. I asked if it was difficult to work and parent at the same time.

"I don't want Jacob to repeat my mistakes," Mandy said. She grabbed two shot glasses from a cupboard near the stove with one hand and placed one in front of me and one in front of her.

"My mom tried to escape some dangerous habits. Even if she was selfish and coddled and neurotic," Mandy said.

"Yeah," I said. I thought about the word coddled and what it implied. My mother had never worked.

I moved the empty beer cans, a dozen and a half scattered on the table. Mandy opened the bottle of Goldschläger and poured some into my shot glass and then into hers. Gold flakes sparkled as they fell from the bottle.

"Thing is," she said, "nobody wants to be their own mother when they have a terrible relationship with her. I could have abandoned Jacob or aborted, but I had to escape what I came from."

She looked behind her towards the bedroom hallway. Then she took my arm and intertwined it with hers, each with our shot glass in hand. Her breath was soft and sour on my face.

"It would be convenient and a lot easier if I just let myself slip into that," she said. "But I have to fight against everything that's encoded in me to be something else."

"No, yeah, that makes sense," I said. Mandy raised her glass.

"To the death of our old selves," she said.

"To the death of our old selves."

We tipped our heads back together and sipped the shot down. Some dribbled out of the sides of my mouth, warm and tingling. She kept her arm intertwined with mine and an embarrassing urge grew for her to hug me. She pressed her body into mine and I tucked my head into the crook of her neck, beneath her chin. She stroked my hair for a second and then pulled away to look at me. I thought she might ask me about my mother, but she didn't. Instead, she kissed me. After that, everything went black.

The day after the fight, I walked with the baby in the stroller. Two young boys played in a front yard as we headed back home, their mothers watching. Ian waved to them, and the older of the two boys, who looked to be four or five, waved back.

"Hey, Lyla!" one mother called. Mandy stood next to the woman. It had been months since I'd seen her. They stood at the edge of the woman's yard, hips cocked, dressed in athleisure.

"Hey!" I said. Mandy introduced me to the woman, Brittney, and I introduced Brittney to the baby. They seemed friendly with each other.

"You've gotten so grown since last I saw you," Mandy said to the baby. It was true. Ian had just been born when we'd gone over for dinner, his eyes hardly able to focus. We texted back and forth a few times after the dinner party, but nothing came of it. The last time I'd texted her, I asked how she was doing, and she replied, "Good." And that was it. She never sent another text.

Brittney's son, Branson, and Mandy's son, Jacob, rode their bikes together.

"Can't wait till he's that age," I said. "More independent."

"You'll miss it," Brittney cooed. "My oldest is sixteen. I haven't been around one this little in so long." Brittney's eyes were rimmed in black and her hair was pulled back into a sleek ponytail.

"May I?" she asked. I hesitated, but before I could stop her, she'd unbuckled his seat and picked him up out of the stroller. I cringed inside, his diaper sogged with piss. Food and snot had collected around the edges of his nose. She held him for a bit, made soft, cooing noises at him. I only noted how cute and lovable Ian was when around people I didn't know.

The girlfriend posted videos of their honeymoon, but each time you viewed one, it would record your username. I created a dummy account and discovered they'd taken their honeymoon to Disneyland. Dozens of pictures showed her posing with her hands placed beneath her chin, her tongue tucked behind her teeth, wearing those characteristic mouse ears. I studied the comedian's smiling face for any sense of false happiness. The rest were just pictures of rides and food—waffles, deep fried cheese, ice cream, hot dogs.

Ian laid down for a nap and I cleaned my floor on my hands and knees with a rag, doing mountain climbers across each portion of the floor. I broke out into a sweat and as I made each pass felt a heightened sense of satisfaction. I checked my phone, wondering if I should log into my throwaway account again, but saw that I had a text from Logan: *be home late again*. Boys shrieked outside, and I peeked through the blinds. Mandy walked up the street with Brittney, talking, and one woman from across the street had joined them. I checked my phone again. Other than Logan, the last text I'd received was from my mother, three days ago. I wondered if I should call her. It was fashionable to complain about motherhood and I didn't want to complain. I wanted to be like my neighbours, whose love and affection looked effortless. And it was hard to determine what was the baby and what was just my life. I had never been happy. Every minor success was like, "That's nice, but what's next?"

I sat down at my laptop and checked the comedian's accounts. He'd kept his own pages private since he'd started dating the girl, but on one account, he'd posted photos from the wedding set to public. There was a snapshot of him in his tux. Him smirking. Them smiling together. Sharing cake. I felt sick at the thought he knew I would look for him, that he'd left his page open for me to find.

I scooped the baby out of his crib, leaving a note to Logan telling him I'd be heading to my mother's. Ian rested against my shoulder as I walked out to the car. I had nothing on my person except my keys, credit card and a cell phone. A case of water sat in the trunk. I buckled Ian into the car seat and drove to the end of the street. Mandy and Brittney waved and I turned right, rolling through the stop sign.

I drove for sixteen hours straight without stopping—except for gas and bathroom breaks.

Ian woke up crying in the backseat as though I'd betrayed him. I kept steady on the road, listened to stacks of CDs, and took an Adderall to keep me awake. My hands trembled when I got to Anaheim. I rolled off the first exit and checked into a hotel near the theme park. The morning sun cut sharp shadows into the parking lot from an enormous sign with plastic pastel-coloured flags that read:

DISNEYLAND
THE HAPPIEST PLACE ON EARTH

I purchased a small bag of toiletries in the hotel lobby and got us settled into our room. I checked social media again to see if the girlfriend had posted any updates but got distracted by a post Logan made from his office. It was a photo of him and his coworkers, making a thumbs-up underneath a piece of graffiti on a wall that said "dicks". I scrolled more, seeing status updates, photos, videos my friends had been sharing. A kaleidoscopic blur. My friends, even my mother, had been living here this whole time, sad and happy and together all at once without telling me a thing. Once I left their pages behind, they were dead to me. No one reached out, so it forced me to reach in.

After the dinner party at Chaz and Mandy's, I woke from my drunkenness next to Logan on their couch, and Mandy was standing there naked with a sand-coloured towel wrapped around her dark hair. She whispered to Logan and me, something about how we had to leave. I rolled over to check the time on my phone. 4 a.m. I hadn't remembered falling asleep. Logan was naked from the waist down. I was still drunk.

"You have to leave," Mandy repeated, "or Chaz says he's leaving me. Get out." I tried to reach into my memory, but only broken images came back. I had an image of Logan walking back into the kitchen as Mandy released me from a kiss. Of me looking in surprise at Logan. Of Mandy on the kitchen table, her legs spread open, with my face in between them.

Later that morning we walked home from the babysitter's and I held the baby in front of me as a kind of shield. "You set me up," I said to Logan. "You knew that I would like her, didn't you?"

"I didn't know any of that would happen," he said. "I know them as well as you do."

Another image came to me once we got home of Logan, standing at the kitchen table while Mandy lay spread-eagled, his taut ass-muscles thrusting into her. I sat back in my chair, silent, as if I were watching someone masturbate.

In the hotel, I turned the TV on and prepared oatmeal for my son. Just an information channel that cycled through the various attractions in Anaheim: the restaurants in Downtown Disney, Adventure City, breweries, ballet. I spooned one last bit of oatmeal into Ian's mouth, wiping up the rest on his chin. I left him on the bed and ran a bath.

The bathroom steamed by the time I got him undressed. The windows had fogged up, but outside it was a clear, blue day. Cicadas and birds sang, and the blurry fronds of palms moved in the wind. I tried to imagine what the comedian and his new wife would do at this moment. I pictured a photo of her hair catching in her smiling teeth from the breeze. Holding hands, taking a shuttle back to their hotel. I waited to hear the ring of my phone, but nothing happened. I then placed two white towels on the toilet-seat lid. When I slipped my pants off, something small and heavy fell out of my pocket and clanged against the floor like change. My wedding ring.

Ian splashed in the water as I opened the small bag of toiletries and pulled out a yellow shaving razor. The bright plastic cracked between my teeth and three thin blades fell into my hand like silver insects. I thought of Mandy, and the many lives I'd lived. If I had known that was the only night I'd spend with her, I might have acted differently. I might not have slept with her. But maybe it didn't matter, the way it didn't matter how hard I tried to not be like my mother. I was cold like her, incapable of letting myself be vulnerable. It was inexcusable. Mandy was right. The only way to avoid becoming your mother is to not become a mother at all.

I got into the bath clothed, clutching the blades, and sat the baby on my lap. I cradled the back of his head with my free hand and held him close, his head underneath my neck. The baby laid his hand on my breast and, drugged by his touch, I thanked Logan, silently, for this special animal he had gifted me.

Ian lifted his head and squeezed his fingers and palm together to mimic waving. I closed my eyes and tried to remember Logan and I in bed the night we made our pact, his hand in mine like a protective, iron lock.

"Baba," my son said.

"Bye-bye," I said. I lay there a long time, skin pink and veins pulsing from the heat, until I could no longer distinguish the sound of his breathing from my own. A terrible noise erupted from my chest as I moved the blade through my skin. The edges of my vision throbbed into a wide blur and Ian crawled, crying, towards the dripping tap. I knew my actions would not free me. Were we not all living this life because we hoped to live another? I'd wind up here again, I was sure of it, having forgotten everything I'd learned.

PUKKAKI

DEFINE HUNGRY

MY NAME IS ON EVERY BILL. This is the order bills are paid:

Rent Electric Gas
Sewer / water
Cell phone (which we share and is the only one in his name but my name is also on it)
Internet
Credit Card (if there's anything left)

I prepay rent and get a few months ahead so I can catch up on school loans. When I have to pay rent again I let the payments in my school loans lapse, but not long enough they send me to collections. The credit card, I let lapse. When I get hungry, I steal.

Initially, it started out as little things. An extra bunch of cilantro, a head of lettuce the cashier forgot to count.

But then they automated the cashier protocol at the local supermarket. Now, instead of ten open cash registers, there were thirty, manned by three people, and only two of them rang the food up themselves. The remaining attendant manned the robot registers, which used the honour system. The remaining registers had you, the customer, do the work. Any idiot with hands can scan a barcode.

Sometimes my stomach growls but my brain says nothing. I feel empty. Weightless and powerful.

I could be hungry like this forever.

I added extra items to my grocery runs just to see what would happen. An avocado or two slipped by undetected. I'd ring up papaya as bananas instead, weighed by the pound, getting them for seventy-five percent off the ticket price.

Then I began slipping bags of shredded cheese and deli meat into the coat pocket of my hoodie. The pocket was too small to fit more stuff, so I ordered this large, lifelike plastic belly from China. I'd walk by and the single attendant would smile at my fake belly and go about her day. People let pregnant women get away with anything. I'd been doing it for months.

Sometimes the hunger is different. It grows. It claws up the back of my neck. I sit, debate about what I want. I could eat something small. Fruit. A salad. Or I could eat my deepest fantasies. Fried butter. Cake donuts. A family pack of chicken nuggets, two large fries and a Diet Coke. A milkshake.

The thing about credit is that interest stacks. With an interest rate at 18.9 percent, you're better off not paying it at all. Just let the thing max itself out. Just let the debt collectors call until it slides off your credit in seven years.

It's not like I'll ever buy a house. Or have children.

Soon, I was slipping a half-dozen avocados, a bag of Roma tomatoes, and garlic cloves into the belly as I walked through produce. I'd put other things in my cart. A bag of mixed salad greens, a wedge of cheesecake, a bag of baby carrots.

The hunger gnaws, incipient and subtle. We see hunger as a separate entity that must be fed; it is not us we are feeding, but the hunger itself. It begs and begs of us until it's satisfied enough to leave us alone. I scroll through high definition pictures of food on my cell phone. The wet drip of lemon frosting off a fluffy poppy seed cake. Creamy horseradish sauce puckering the soft side of a steaming hamburger bun.

The most expensive food I saved for the fake belly. Cans of caviar, sardines, smoked oysters. Paté and fancy crackers made entirely of cheese. I'd walk up to the self-checkout, and ring up my items, smiling at the attendant. Sometimes, they'd ask when I was due, the sardine cans slipping between the avocados, the tomatoes bruising against my ribs.

After rent, utilities, and internet, there's enough money left to last us for three weeks' worth of food, if we eat three square meals a day and measure our proportions perfectly. Unless Erik's mother sends us an envelope full of branded gift cards. In that case, we end up eating out for the last week of the month, until the next paycheck comes in.

The pictures of food eventually aren't enough. The hunger pulls until it's not hunger anymore. Something takes over. The fantasy, my brain decides, must become reality.

A lot of my late night binges, they go on the credit card. Fifteen bucks here or there becomes forty on a good night. Sometimes I hit up three drive-thrus on my way home before stopping in the parking lot of the supermarket and idling my car for twenty minutes as I eat everything I ordered.

A pink credit card statement sits on the passenger seat of my car. It's asking for $25. *If you pay this amount every month, you will finish paying off your debt in thirty-five years.* At five thousand dollars in debt, you can expect to pay that off by the time you retire, paying 138 times more into interest than you initially owed.

In the past year alone, I've thrown up at least five thousand dollars' worth of food. Body by bulimia.

The headlines I pray to see:
Federal Government Forgives All Student Loan Debt Universal Basic Income Begins In Select Cities Across U.S.

Tonight is special. Erik's birthday. I walk in to the store wearing a muumuu and the pregnancy belly and do my usual routine. Through the produce, I grab a bag of salad greens, a tomato, a pineapple. A package of pea shoots. Then I wander through the aisles until I get to the frozen section.

Eventually, the credit card company will sell your debt to a debt collector. Money that doesn't exist gets sold to a company whose job it is to reacquire that money. They hire people that get paid, per letter and phone call, to collect it. The letters go from pink to red. The ice cream cake is on the bottom shelf of the freezer. It works to my advantage. I swing the door of the freezer and hold it open with my cart. I pull the elastic of the belly taut as far as it will go. A strap breaks on one side. With the other hand, I pick up the box of cake from the bottom and then scoot it upwards, underneath the blue Hawaiian-print muumuu, in between the belly and my stomach.

"Ma'am?" an attendant in a red shirt and khaki pants asks from the other end of the aisle.

My skin screams from the cold.

The people collecting debt are as hungry as you are. Motivated by the same economy.

In the dumpster behind the store, day old bread sits in plastic bags. It would be impossible to starve in America if the grocery store didn't bolt and lock their garbage.

The cake burns my skin and I can already feel my tongue spreading the cake apart where it meets the ice cream. The frosting melting against my lips.

One of the headlines Erik and I read to each other last week: *Man Stabbed Female Debt Collector to Death in Indianapolis.*

"Do you need any help?" the attendant asks. She's approaching me now.

"Just catching my breath," I say.

Slowly, I stand, one hand inside of the muumuu, which now extends a whole foot in front of me, holding the cake from the bottom.

"Are you sure?" she asks.

I push my cart away with one hand to the other end of the aisle, my breath sharp from the icy box. The cake is melting. I want to slather myself in it. The box squishes against the fake belly, against my stomach, and something wet drips between my legs.

Sometimes, debt collectors will pose as family or friends to figure out where you live. They'll find your address from voter registration. Driver's licenses. Social media. The only way to avoid it is to go off grid.

The attendant approaches me. Frosting leaks from the box. I can see myself at home, half the cake in my stomach, its soft slide back up my throat.

I suck air between my teeth, with one hand beneath my belly and the other on the cart. I waddle as fast as I can to check out, sneakers squeaking on the liquid dripping from my belly. Another attendant steps in front of me as I make it to the self-checkout lane.

To stop the collection calls, I could go off grid. Stop voting. Leave an old address on my driver's license. I would lose everything—all my followers online.

My confidence dips. The attendant, her blue smock covered in stains, makes a concerned face and looks towards my feet.

"Ma'am, let me help you with that," she says. She motions to the cart.

Wet vanilla drips from my knees.

One day, someone from a number you don't recognise might call and ask you to do a survey. He might ask you a few questions to get you to elicit some basic information. And when he has enough, he calls your bank, pretending to be you. He gets your personal information from the bank. And suddenly, the red letters show up again.

My heart leaps.

"I got it—" I say. I move my hand, and the cake shifts. My fake belly shudders as another strap snaps, and I grab it to hold it in place.

"Ma'am—?"

I take off running, leaving the cart behind. I slip once, twice on the ice cream as I make a break for the front door and catch myself. Another attendant, an old man with a smiley face sticker plastered onto his name badge, puts his arms out. A third attendant runs towards me. The smell of vanilla rises from the muumuu. I can make it.

It's just a transaction. I left a dozen eggs behind once.

I deserve this.

THANK YOU, LAUREN GREENFIELD

SOME OF MY EARLIEST MEMORIES are of feeling bad. In third grade, the teacher passed around batteries for a science experiment. I don't remember the science experiment. It seemed like we were all going to do the same thing, but the batteries being handed out were a mix of 9-Volt and smaller, double-A batteries. I got the smaller batteries, and cried because it seemed as though I was being singled out. I had the impression the smaller batteries meant my project would not be as good.

An earlier memory, from kindergarten, was in PE. Everyone in the class had to roll from one side of the gym to the other on little blue scooter boards. I wore a pink frilly dress. It kept getting stuck under the wheels of the scooter, so I was slow and got stuck in the middle of the gym. I began scream-crying because I was left behind. Everyone else had made it to the other side. I don't remember how long I was left there to cry.

Some time after, I stopped wearing dresses. I'd wear shorts and white t-shirts to school, and other kids made fun of me for having chicken legs and knobby knees. I was too thin, I guess, for an eight year old.

But being too thin is like being too drunk. Which is to say, it's not that much of a problem.

/

Maybe I've always been taught to see my depression as selfish.

How pretentious can we get?

I recently bought myself a flip phone. The kind with flat buttons and no internet access. It keeps me off social media, and also keeps me from obsessively searching for images of early 2000s era "scary skinny" pop stars. The quintessential Mary Kate, post-Simple Life Nicole Richie. Also Paris Hilton, Tara Reid, Mischa Barton. Portia De Rossi. In the early half of the decade, pop magazines were obsessed with the phrase "scary skinny."

I am trying to assess if my current obsession with the late nineties and early 2000s is due to my desire to escape the current time. (Used to be also obsessed with the idea of dating a man who drives a gold Corolla).

I am never not myself (which is painful) and I am simultaneously never able to be myself (which is also painful). When I'm hungry I imagine my body is eating itself and it relaxes me.

/

I had sex today which proves that I can starve myself and still have sex.

I am constantly working to prove that starving does not fuck up necessary shit in my life like the functioning of my libido or the way I connect to people.

I am trying to convince myself my decision to buy a flip phone was for mental health reasons and not out of a compulsive desire to consume.

I can't sleep.

I am wearing gold adidas. I am in a gold Corolla. I am dreaming about these things.

/

I spend most of my time at night rereading my own experiences. I feel so far from myself or I am trying hard to imagine how you might experience my life, how I or my art might be experienced in your eyes.

Of course I know this is impossible and you will lie to me if I ask you about your experience of me. It also feels self involved to ask you about the ways in which I interest you.

NUDES

I am not ready to discuss how self involved I am.

(Curious about the kind of car you drive and whether or not the car is a manual. Is the car rear wheel drive, is it older than 1992?)

/

I have decided I have late capitalist bulimia in which I purchase many things quickly and then almost immediately regret having consumed these things. I attempt to rid my self of these regrets as quickly as possible by donating old clothes and items that are similar to the items I have purchased in order to assuage the guilt I have contributed to this system.

I also might have actual bulimia.

I re-watched this documentary from my teenage years called THIN, which came out in 2005. Periodically I research the young women profiled from Renfrew, considered one of the most famous inpatient eating disorder clinics in the country, to see how they've survived. My favourite one committed suicide in 2008. My other favourite, the twin, made a blog post, also in 2008, then disappeared for a while. I have watched this movie so many times it reels in my head. I have searched for the young women many times.

When I am not sick, I know not to watch it. Like reading *Wasted: A Memoir*, I know exactly why I watch it and what I am looking for. There is a scene in the movie I can recall with particular clarity: one of the thinnest girls (who is also profiled in the hardbound picture book which accompanies the movie) cries during a group therapy session. She's in her early or late twenties. She is attempting to warn a much younger girl, sixteen, by describing the experience of bringing "pre-packaged meals" to Thanksgiving dinner, and the separation of eating, of being unable to eat what her family eats, brings her to tears when she describes it. The hair rises on the back of my neck. It fills me with adrenaline, to think about the times I have spent with my family eating separate holiday meals, meals I made just for me, with each calorie counted exactly as it needs to be, to think about the holidays I couldn't eat separately and so gorged myself gleefully on gravy and potatoes and meat before stealing away to the bathroom, where I had to figure out the most silent way to purge in a relative's house where every footstep echoed.

Am I romanticising the sickest parts of myself? Is this why I believe recovery to be false?

/

I'm attending Alcoholics Anonymous to seek therapy for my eating disorder, on Mondays at noon when my partner is at work, so I won't have to tell him I am going.

Sometimes throwing up feels as good as or better than sex because it is extremely personal and ritualised. It is easier for me to vomit when it's forced than when my body naturally attempts to vomit on its own from nausea or sickness.

Lately, I do not want to have sex because I am low energy and the sex seems to be more about the other person rather than about me.

93

NUDES

The girl from THIN who killed herself purged, too. I am not sure if she considered herself bulimic. There is volatility in purging food, in bulimia, that does not exist within the actions of anorexia. I felt most suicidal when I was purging every day, when it felt that any food in my body was an invasion I kept forcing upon myself.

My partner does not know I have relapsed.

There is a kind of shame in being bulimic versus being anorexic, even when you are a very thin bulimic. As though there is an unwanted feminine chaos that exists within bulimia.

I mean that anorexia is seen as the ideal because it is controlled. It is why the most common depiction of eating disorders on television are of anorexics. As I restrict my intake and attempt to become the idealised version of my self (which is, however, not the idealised version of how society believes women should be), eventually my body can no longer restrict. It can take days to get to this point, or months. I then, unwillingly and also willingly, consume as many calories as possible. I expunge them from my body. The truth comes out: I cannot be controlled. I am actually messy. A garbage person, eating garbage things, and then wasting them. Anorexia is the organised, rational masculine ideal to my unwanted feminine chaos. Maybe that is why it is the more idolised and more glamorised disorder. Maybe that is why bulimics are not seen but instead heard.

Forcing myself—to do anything, even what I ultimately want—is something I am used to doing in all of my relationships, including the one I have with myself.

/

AA meetings are the safest to attend because thin women don't bother me but eating disordered women will make me want to vomit or starve.

If I went to an eating disorder programme, I would be pleased because I could revel in my sickness. I would get sicker, even if I gained weight. Weight gain seems to be the only factor, or at least the main factor, in what recovery looks like to eating disorder programs.

There is a tendency for anorexics to be extremely proud of their ability to hurt themselves in such a controlled and sustained manner.

/

The girl from THIN who committed suicide was kicked out of Renfrew because she violated community rules. The therapists and administration called her "tricky". They said they didn't trust her. At the beginning of her stay, she pocketed anti-anxiety medication to give to the twin, who hid it in her room. They found the medication during a room check, and determined this was a violation. Then, they learned the girl got a tattoo during an unsupervised outing, which was also a violation.

I am inclined to believe another factor in her expulsion is because her weight had stabilised. It was, at least, more stable than other patients. Her insurance had run out, and her mother begged the hospital staff to keep her for another week. The father was footing the bill. The mother said to the hospital staff, *This is it for her.* The mother said her father would not fund another stay like this again, and there was no one in her home state who could help her the way Renfrew could.

I would be interested to know, if she had been more skeletal, how they would have weighed the decision to kick her out. With eating disorders, what factors determine how sick a person is? Is it how I see myself, or is it how you see me?

/

I am interested in the shape of my thighs when they are around my partner's waist. They have changed sizes many times. Sometimes his eyes draw to my thigh gap.

I think he prefers them when they are at their smallest and I prefer them that way, too.

I hate how every time I decide to recover and eat a normal amount I immediately regret my decision to be so square. I bargain with myself: some people drink alcohol to forget. Some people gamble. Some people smoke. Maybe my smoking is that I stop eating, or eat too much and purge. My vice could be that simple if I let it.

The truth, though, is that it is not simple. It gets out of hand, it causes problems.

I tell myself I should become a nutritionist so I can always be surrounded by the sickness of others. I could openly obsess about numbers, macros and nutrients. It would give me an excuse to continue unhealthy eating patterns masked as healthy, because I would have to do it for work.

They say psychologists study and become psychologists because they are crazy and trying to fix themselves. The level of food obsession in nutritionists I have met makes me assume the same is true. The cross section between therapist and nutritionist must exist: they are trying to convince themselves they're fine while drenching themselves in the environment of other sick people needing to be fixed. I smell, taste, touch the atmosphere of anorexia and I immediately miss everything about it.

A neatly arranged plate of crudités, cutting fruit in half and saving the rest for later, black coffee, high fiber cereal. The way my calves get stretched in long, 3 p.m. shadows when I take a walk. Pants tight enough to make that little concave void between my legs.

/

I am always guarded.

I still have not told my partner about the AA meetings. If I tell him about the AA meetings, it will imply I have a problem with alcohol when I do not (and if I tell him it is for my relapse, he will know, then, that I have relapsed).

I make the assumption he does not want me to have a problem with alcohol because it seems to be a large part of our lives.

However, I would rather be around alcohol addicts than purgers or starvers because addiction seems to be the root of the issue. Although I have abused alcohol to lose weight (why eat when you can drink) and have put myself into alcoholic ketoacidosis (alcohol lowers your blood sugar, but if there's no glucose in your system, the body can shut down) twice trying to lose weight, I do not consider myself an alcoholic or wanting to revel in the sickness of alcohol addiction. I am addicted to bodies. I am addicted to consuming bodies. I am addicted to my body, comparing my body to other sick bodies. I am addicted to consuming things and then ridding myself of them.

I sent a version of this essay to my close friend and mentor and she said, *It seems you may be addicted to addiction. To identifying as an addict.* Perhaps what makes recovery so square is it implies I would no longer harbour a sense of obsession within me. For many years I have felt obsession is the engine with which I move. I enjoy it. It feels good, deliciously painful, to obsess. Especially over things I cannot control.

I am very proud of how much vomit is expelled from my body.

/

My partner's ex-girlfriend was anorexic and she was also, at one point, my best friend.

It is unfair of me to say my partner prefers my thighs when they are smaller. I know I am projecting my own tastes onto him as a way to continue being sick, as a way to continue a nonexistent competition with my once best friend.

Alcoholic ketoacidosis starts as a slow-meld out of body experience. Your systems begin to slow. There is a throbbing. A sense that your mind is living, but your meat package is about to burst. I felt scared at the time, but now I look back on it and think, it could have been peaceful.

When I say 'best friend' what I mean is we starved together for several years and got to our lowest weights together, before the two were ever dating. It was very romantic. Meaning I romanticised it heavily.

The girl from THIN who committed suicide never revealed her tattoo to the Renfrew staff. The tattoo was on her hip, a half-circle, hugged by a swooping, long line; the symbol of eating disorder recovery.

Sometimes my partner forgets to eat.

/

I forgot about the gold Corolla.

You do not forget a romance like one that involves your favourite sickness.

The twin I loved from THIN has a Facebook profile. I found it last month on my hours long research binge while re-watching the documentary. I was convincing myself treatment wasn't necessary or that I could sustain this behaviour of restricting my calorie intake until it was impossible to fight and then binge eating and purging to compensate. On the Facebook profile, the only public information the twin revealed was a life event. She'd become an eating disorder counselor at a recovery clinic.

Her profile photo is a very thin body in a very fitted dress.

WE ARE SHARP EDGES BUMPING AGAINST EACH OTHER

I SEE THE GRID of city through the airplane window. Then suddenly there is no grid, but an indeterminate amount of sky and water. There's an energy I can't tap into. Negative space in my mind or surrounding my body, unsure which. I think about writing or doing something productive and the eating disorder latches on instead, filling the emptiness with thoughts of my body or food. I walk down the aisle of the airplane to the restroom and close the door. The girl in the mirror contorts into strange shapes, first her kneecaps touch then she bends her hips back slightly. A gap three fingers wide appears between her thighs and I think: I'm still normal yet, I haven't forsaken the two months I spent losing weight from two days of overeating.

The girl in the mirror unzips her pants.

The girl in the mirror wraps her fingers around her upper arms.

The girl in the mirror sits on the toilet and stares at pictures of the girl in the mirror on her phone.

The girl in the phone is doing the same thing, contorting her body, in countless other mirrors she encounters, as though pieces of her are left in each mirrored place.

/

Everything is fine as long as we're fucking. The relationship becomes fucked when he forgets to tell me what to do. He forgets I am trying my best to perform for him.

/

One of the symptoms of borderline personality disorder is 'chronic emptiness'. I learned this because I was typing the phrase "i feel dead inside" into google every other day to find a way to fix myself. I rephrased it over and over so I could avoid finding reddit threads full of edgelords and find something closer to my actual lived experience. Eventually, something popped up about this illness.

I question the existence of this illness the way many do because of *Girl, Interrupted*. More people have seen the movie than the book. They see Winona's short-cropped hair and Angie's chopped bangs. The image of her with a pen at her neck, ready to stab it in. As a teen, I coveted her fucked up coolness. I've grown up into it, though now I dread what I've become. Not damaged enough to be placed in a 72-hour hold, but damaged enough that I struggle with basic life tasks. I have not read the book. I assume many people think the illness is not real, but that is because my partner doesn't think it's real, and I have a problem with assuming he's the master of my world.

/

Imagine a world where all your thoughts were searchable like web history.

/

I want to stay sick because it feels good until it no longer feels good.

I want to become healthy because staying sick makes me feel cruel and selfish.

On Saturday night, I got medium-drunk at a bar with my old man. We went home. It was an uneventful night but I drank my last double neat and felt like a badass.

I got home and rubbed against his warm body in bed and we had sex in a way that felt like I wanted to have it. It had been a few months since I'd initiated this way. Or even wanted to. I felt like I wanted to.

/

He says a word like "codependence". He says it when he talks about other women. He says it when we fight. It doesn't matter in what context. The finger in my brain points to a chalkboard that says, "This is what codependence is."

But my brain doesn't understand. It is reaching inside itself, looking for knowledge, shuffling through my experiences, to place the word's meaning.

Nothing is inside my brain anymore.

I *know* I have experience with codependence and have understood what codependence is in the past. But right now the finger in my brain points to a word like codependence and nothing is there. So it reaches past it, examining imitations of those lost feelings. I need to express I understand what he says, without revealing I have no emotional or mental reaction. I don't know my own emotions anymore. I just recognise what he wants, and articulate it.

I am afraid to tell him that I do not feel things right now.

I am afraid it will mean the things I gave up to get better were for nothing. I left my job and made things harder on him financially and it didn't make things better.

I recognise I am more content and less stressed. But the emptiness is there.

/

Emptiness is both nothing and something.

Emptiness takes up no space. But it sucks up all the space, as well.

/

Women are loud with their *mouths*. Men are loud by *existing*.

/

I posted a picture of a youtube video on my instagram. It listed four of the nine symptoms of borderline personality disorder.
- intense mood swings
- problems with self-worth
- unstable interpersonal relationships
- impulsive, self-destructive behavior

I captioned the photo with the phrase 'are there people who aren't like this.' Someone, I don't remember who, commented 'right? these are such generic characteristics.'

The depth to which these behaviours describe my own makes me question whether I have this personality disorder. How generic are my character traits? If they are so generic, why do they seem to fit me so neatly?

/

My brain is a layer cake. Where I am most like myself is the bottom-most layer. The top layers are filled with symbols, patterns, and acknowledged language so I can replicate a person living in society.

Alcohol eats through all that. It soaks through all those top layers, so I can touch the part of myself I leave unseen or have trouble accessing. Another me is inside of me, a real me I can't remember. My mind remembers it, but I don't. For example, I am afraid of lightning, but I don't know why. I believe on a single dark day it will come down for me, for all the sins I have performed. When I am hungover I listen to classical music and it is only then I realise how overwhelming and commercialised the world is.

NUDES

/

All I feel is my teeth grinding down until my jaw aches. Until the roots of my teeth are raw.

/

Do you think my hunger for attention online mirrors the attention-seeking behaviours of a person with borderline personality disorder, and if so, how has technology changed the way we interact with our illnesses?

/

I put my arm on the corner of the table then I grabbed a bottle of conditioner then I slammed the conditioner against my arm until the skin split against the wood corner.

/

To write about eating disorders you must have good bone structure. You need to, because as soon as you say this: *i used to have an eating disorder,* the whole of their eyes will roll toward your feet, examine the width of the gap between your thighs, the protrusions of your breasts and belly. They will wonder, where was the skeleton that once resided here?

/

The girl in the mirror is back again but she is bigger now. A bruise blossoms on her left, or maybe it's her right, arm. It is hard to say which. The only thing that has shrunk is her thigh gap.

"You still have a thigh gap" is what he says, as if his opinion has any bearing on how the girl in the mirror should look. Only the girl in the mirror can determine when she is happy with herself, and the answer to when is never.

The girl in the mirror rounds her palms across the thick skin of her ass cheeks. The body, like most things, is amoral. The body, like most things, is a tool. The body's morality depends on its user. The body's morality is determined by the types and amounts of consumption it participates in. The body is a filter. The body is a filter for language. The body is a filter for reality, which it distills into image. The body filters image. The body is an image. The body is image.

The girl in the mirror finds femur meeting pelvis, separated by several inches of meat. The ass is like an empty bag. The ass-skin gives, it feels delicate and crepey in that unique, deflated-body way. She massages the empty bag, the curious way the meat was inside it then was suddenly not. She wonders how he feels when he grabs this empty ass-bag, also, like a balloon filled with smooth sand.

In the mirror, she bends over and looks for the curve of the iliac crest, which is now covered with a layer of thick, firm meat. Today is not the day that she will see it. The girl faces the mirror again and presses her pelvis towards the wall behind her, to see the space between her legs. The space between her legs is where a thousand moments lie.

LIVESTREAM

I MADE PLANS TO DRIVE to my parents' house in Bend, Oregon, a dirty white clapboard on the corner of a street with no name and miles of wired fence. I drive through Nebraska, I drive through Colorado, I drive through Wyoming and Montana. Between Denver and Bozeman there is nothing, a big nothing. The sky is filament above me.

Bozeman is my stop for the night. Main Street is a slip off the highway and a slip back on and in any other moment the town would be gone in an instant. I get out at a rest stop and look at the sky, the impossible sky, which hangs higher than it seems in other places, as if the glass that makes the atmosphere keeps the clouds further away from the ground. Everything around tinged pale yellow from the setting sun. A man at the rest stop takes a second glance and I wipe soured milk from the sides of my mouth, dust crumbs from my abdomen. I think of myself as a single mother already, conscious of my youth, my round belly

109

accentuating the youth of my soft cheeks. I am only slightly showing. In my car, remnants of the trip: crusted coffee cups, food trash, a bottle of vitamins on the seat, a duffel bag with the insides spilling out.

In the parking lot of an Australian steakhouse franchise, I turn off the car and the heat wraps around me like sheet plastic. Other cars pull in, people amble towards the entrance.

The hostess is my age, shoulder length brown hair, wide hips, smooth skin. She taps her pen against a clipboard as she asks if anyone else will be joining me. I say no. She keeps tapping and looks down at a map of the restaurant. My lips are chapped; I bring my hand to my mouth again. I imagine the feel of her lips parting as the tips of my fingers graze against dried lip-skin. Some part of me wants to ask her for a job application. The foyer is air conditioned and I rub my shoulders pink.

She sits me at a booth and gives me a large, laminated menu. I watch as the lint on the back of her black trousers sashays away. I fantasise about what it would be like to stay in Bozeman, to live her life. I wonder if it is better or different than mine, if she is dating anyone. If her parents are nice. If she thinks about the future.

Of course she does all of these things. I take a sip of ice water, my hand wet with condensation, and think about who I have left behind: a man I thought I loved. I wear a ring on my finger, but we haven't married. I am supposed to be planning a wedding. I am supposed to be *in love*. I am supposed to stop lying about how I pay the bills. Instead I leave the apartment in the middle of the night, I turn my phone on airplane mode just to disappear off the grid for a few hours. I wake up in the bed of an ex who burns me mixed CDs before placing a white envelope into my purse. In bed, the ex rubs my belly, not knowing who resides beneath.

I trace my hands over the sweaty plastic of the menu, touching perfect beef, a fluffed mashed potato, a wedge of moist cheesecake. Slats of light glare across my table, shift, and then disappear. A waitress walks away from the window directly in front of me, the chain waving from touch. The outline of an industrial park is a burned shadow in the blinds.

My future now stands before me like a city of tall buildings. Everything is already built. There is no changing the location of skyscrapers. I can see them in the distance. One building is the birth process, the pain and fear of the unknown; one building is a career path; one building is a job with no upward mobility; one building is retirement and savings; one is my relationship with _____.

One building is a mortgage, yet another terrifying building is the health of my aging parents, the decreasing lucidity of my mother. The tallest building is the child itself, as it will become the singular responsibility that will define my life.

I order perfect beef with a forty-four ounce caramel-coloured diet soda and a baked potato with butter, sour cream, bacon. I drink down the complimentary glass of water. I stare at my cell phone, navigate to one social media site after another, post updates about scheduling a livestream. The waitress brings my meal and smiles at me with lipstick on her teeth and I smile back wishing I could be her friend, wishing I could rent a hotel room here and never leave.

I could do whatever I wanted, but I don't.

I sit my cell phone up against the frosted glass of soda, camera pointed on my meal, the little red light on the screen flashing, numbers counting up to one minute, then one minute and a half, then two minutes, then two and a half.

Meal is such a disgusting word to describe the act of eating.

NUDES

I eat cubes of steak, the potato next, then broccoli, washed down with another glass of water, pause the video, drink the diet soda, and leave cash on the table.

The restroom door is heavy and the lacquer is tacky against my hands, fluorescent light reflected on the beige tiles inside, a geometric row of stalls. The lights flicker like a fly beating its wings and it is as though I can see and I cannot see at the same time. Like a dream. I lock the door behind me in the stall, having to lift and place the door shut. I place my cell phone on the stainless steel receptacle for sanitary napkins and tampons and un-pause the livestream. I look at the camera without speaking, smile and remember the porn star I watched the night before at a motel in Colorado Springs, how she got choke-fucked in the face by some nameless, disposable pair of legs with a dick attached, her mascara smeared into the creases of her eyes, and every time she vomited (did she have a gag reflex, still, after all of that?), the useless pair of legs would produce an arm that swept up all of the spit and vomit and slapped it onto her face. Her pigtails torn and pulled, she sat there, a moment of hesitation before placing her fake nail to her mouth, Cali-fornia-bright teeth glaring as her lips split into a smile. I smile for the camera this way, push fingers down my throat, reach for the reflex.

The sound of a cartoon coin being collected rings from the phone. I am getting tipped. Every tip nets fifty cents to a couple of dollars. I have to push harder and harder into my throat, the reflex dying from overuse, leaving teeth marks on my knuckles, the two fingers flailing harder inside the spitty cave of my throat.

I look from the toilet to the phone and bloodshot eyes meet me, my hand fisting my mouth, chats floating in and out of existence. More tips ring. Everything kicks and I push harder, and it kicks, empty, like a hiccup, and I push harder, my abdomen squeezing, and I wonder about the fetus inside, if it feels hugged and warm, and then everything comes up in hard, square chunks: the broccoli, raw and confetti like, the potatoes in solid lumps, sticking to everything. My eyes sparkle and blink. More anonymous tips. More tips. More tips.

I think of _____.

The single ply toilet paper crumbs from my fists like sunburn skin. I turn off the livestream, and stand up to wash my hands. When I open the bathroom door, the hostess is standing at the sink, but seems surprised, as if she hadn't known I was there. I imagine her waiting for me, leaning against the wall, listening to the retching sounds and cartoon coin drops pinging every few seconds. She dries her hands and leaves the bathroom without making eye contact. I walk to my car and check my account and tally the tips, but it is not enough to score a room for the night. Back on the road a storm threatens to burst and I find a truck stop somewhere between Bozeman and Idaho Springs. I park the car on the dark side of the gas station, the clouds flickering above, thunder a distant gurgle. I press my hands into my stomach, the bulb of growth inside me, and feel as empty as the sky.

MONEY
SHOT

OFF SCREEN
I ACHE

HE MOVES AND I LIE STILL, eyes at the ceiling. What my mother taught me was that we could do a lot of nothing. We could close our mouths, our legs, our hearts and men like my father might stick around for twenty-six years. Before they decide that what they miss most is a woman who speaks, who runs, whose heart beats faster when they're near. Maybe a man like Gavin would stick around, too.

My film body writhes across computer screens. That body doesn't breathe on TV. Gavin sticks his fingers in my mouth and I roll my tongue across his finger skin, pushing them to my palate. When I grab Gavin's wrist, he draws his fingers out but I push his hand further in, let my jaw hang. My cheeks swell with spit. The pads of his fingers caress the mealy bumps of my far-back tongue. His palm is humid and spicy.

Sometimes I forget I am woman and think I am human. Or perhaps a bird. Feathers sprout from my wrists and I spread my wings to escape this salted earth and out of nowhere the crack of my neck against a cover startles me awake. I've created carefully constructed boxes of how a person should live her life and I'm terrified to rise out.

The weak membrane of my lip rolls between his knuckle and my top teeth as his first two fingers curl into my throat. The whole of his hand grasps deep until something sharp splits against my lip. A snap, then wet warm release like pissing in a hot tub. I suck spit. It trickles down my chin. Gavin slips his hand out and clear, red threads string between us.

I tongue where my incisor was and pain jolts through my upper jaw and into my nose. Half a tooth falls in my hand, a cracked ivory shard with a gnarled nerve inside. The soft gummy spot tastes like a penny. I try to put the tooth back in its space. Each tooth around the broken one dislodges, one by one, like a breaking bridge. I stare at Gavin and he glances at his hand, then looks away. I rustle them around my palms, my teeth like golden nuggets. This bloodshine mouthpit in their place.

A DEEP WELL

I GUESS I SHOULD GET TO the incident with the gun.
Our life before the incident was full of parties, drinking, playing
poker for cigarettes. At the first party Daddy took me to I sat
on the arm of his chair while a girl asked me who I was, what
I did. I felt shy, threatened by her beauty and her relationship to
Daddy—I made up different scenarios, that perhaps they'd fucked
before or kissed or at least shot-gunned weed. I walked onto the
patio to smoke. Four men played poker for cigarettes on a frost-
ed-glass top patio table, a mélange of Kools, Camels and Pall Malls
all piled in the middle. Daddy came outside and the sound of
Tech-Nine echoed and muted as he let the door close behind
him. He placed his hand at the small of my back and we joined the
poker players at the table. I was more comfortable out here with
Daddy and the other men. The women wore dresses that swung
from their hips and had straightened their hair. A stocky man
wearing a white t-shirt and black Dickies tossed me a few cards.
The assortment seemed random to me so I aimed on collecting
colours; that seemed right. When we revealed our hands, I laid
mine out and looked at everyone's else's, all indiscernible to me.

"Is this anything?" I asked. Daddy slapped the table, laughing. The other men roared with laughter, too. I hid my face in my hair. "I don't know how to play."

Daddy touched my arm. "Girly, you just won." He slid the pile of cigarettes into a gallon-size Ziplock bag. "That's a flush." It was enough for a week or more between the two of us—a whole carton.

After the party, I stayed at his apartment for a few weeks. When I think of our time in his studio, he had very little belongings. A bed, an entertainment centre, a TV and a gaming console. He played war games all night, slept all day. When he was high, he wanted to hold my hand and lay his head in my lap, ask me questions about my dreams or plans. They all included him. Then we walked to the grocery store and got whatever we could afford to eat for the night, sometimes just apples, cheese, a loaf of bread. Once, he made me miso soup. He began smoking weed constantly—not a second without it. On the twelfth consecutive day of being high, he woke up at 4 p.m., smoked a bowl, and left the room to brush his teeth. The shower faucet turned on. I scrolled through news on my phone, not paying much attention. He yelled my name from the shower.

"I'm staring at the tile," he said, "and a portal to hell has opened up. Daisy, how long have I been here? Will I ever come back?"

Four days later, he felt sober again. After that he didn't smoke anymore.

A couple times, neighbours called the cops on us for our parties. You'd hear everything through the walls. At 3 a.m., Officer Halstead came and told us to keep it down. A group of us

had been singing "Wrecking Ball" by Miley Cyrus at the top of our lungs.

Everything was good with Daddy. We drank and drank, and had parties on the weekends. Full-time employment was difficult for him for several reasons I can't divulge.

Daddy must have anticipated the change that had to come, but maybe he wasn't ready. I had to stop drinking. It was a morning I had to be at work at 5 a.m. to open. It didn't matter where, all those jobs were the same. I woke up at 3:45 to shower, and when I checked the date on my phone, I'd realised something felt off. I pulled back the shower curtain and found Daddy in the tub, his gun held tight to his chest, empty beer bottles in his lap.

He took a pull of his beer, and it reminded me of the darkness that lingered in him. We were bound now and yet I knew of his past, the potential for future grief. Daddy would always be unstable. He was sad and his sadness manifested as anger. When I think of it now, the stability, what I could have had, something hardens in me. At one point in my life I may have cried, but now I don't anymore. I know what I have chosen.

I was tired. And a little nauseous. Daddy offered me a beer.

"I'm pregnant," I said. I hadn't bled in two months, had somehow missed it. My stomach distended sorely. I didn't need a test. Daddy shifted in the tub, and a jealous throb rang through my ears. I could no longer be complicit in his ability to commiserate through drinking.

"A baby is such an abstract thing before you have it," my mother once said. "But you give birth to it, and this thing becomes *your baby*. A hole the size of a grave widens between you and your friends and in the grave is your child-free past. Gone."

Daddy swilled the liquid around in his beer bottle.

The nausea lurched towards my throat. "I'll leave you to it," I said.

"Are you going back to sleep?" he asked. His speech slurred.

I nodded. "I'll call in to work." The warmth of his flannel comforted me when I leaned to kiss him on the forehead. He put a hand on my stomach and left it there for a moment. I had a feeling everything was going to be okay.

I left and crawled back into his bed—a mattress on the floor. The sky greyed through the windows, and the radiator hissed on. I was happy to be alone for a while. Soon I would never be alone again. I placed my hands at the flattest part of my body, right beneath my ribs.

My stomach rounded up a little, but only on one side. I placed my hand on the firm lump. I imagined it growing, able to receive all it needed. This small human in my charge could die. Part of me was also dying. The internet told me the baby was the size of an olive. Somehow, it seemed so much larger already.

Out of the dark, I heard what sounded like a heavy plank of wood fall against a floor. I knew immediately what it was. I waited for scuffling, or screaming. The moment stretched and my heart beat heavy patterns into the silence around my ears. I dialed 911, but did not call. I hid beneath the sheets, instead, waiting.

The last time I had done this, Daddy and his friend Jeff had stayed up drinking, like any normal night. I woke to fighting. They moved across the apartment and I noticed the friend wasn't playful, this time. Jeff had become belligerent, too drunk to realise. Later, Daddy said he thought he might have to kill Jeff that night. Something turned in him, some raw, angry thing had been let out, something that had been holed up for a long time. Jeff wasn't letting up, and Daddy moved into a guillotine pose to choke him out. Daddy tried to subdue him and failed at first. He rolled and got him in something that looked like a cradle hold. His face was red and wet with spit. I hid in the bathroom, wondering if I would have to grab the gun. Jeff packed, too, and for the first time in my life I feared what it meant to have a gun in the apartment.

Footsteps rang from the bathroom and the door burst open to a glowing silhouette of Daddy, the pistol in his hand. His hair was ragged. He gripped a pulsing dark spot at his abdomen.

"I'm sorry," he slurred. He took a step closer and I jumped out of bed, ran towards him. His eyes were tight pinpricks of fear.

"What happened?" I asked.

"I'm sorry. I'm so sorry," he said again. I placed my hand on his gut and took Daddy to the bed. We lay there in the dark. He put his hands on me in protective places, one over my stomach, and one on the side of my cheek. His mouth hovered close to mine. The purposeful in-out of his breath at my lips.

"I can't stop making bad decisions," he said, in a low whisper. "I keep trying to do the right thing, but each step I take seems to be a wrong turn."

"You don't make bad decisions," I said, trying to pull him from the bed.

"The gun isn't legal," he said. He went deadweight.

An urgent dread filled my lungs and I breathed the way I'd learned from watching pregnancy videos, "Hehe, hoo," as I struggled to get my foot through the bottom of my pants. I looked for my sneakers, and slipped my feet into them, sockless.

NUDES

I threw a faux fur coat on over my pyjamas and tied my hair up into a pony tail.

Daddy turned off the lights, leaving a splotch of blood on the switch. By the front door, I noticed it: a small bullet hole in the ceiling, and two smaller holes in the wall near it.

"I'm sorry we have to do this, I just keep making bad decisions."

I led him out the front door and locked the apartment. We rushed down the stairs towards the car. My foot caught a banister on way down, and we tumbled forward to the landing. For a split second we both were weightless. I thought of the grave then, a deep well, each new moment a handful of dirt being thrown inside.

SURVIVALIST

(with elizabeth ellen)

YOU CAN'T ASK ME THOSE QUESTIONS, if I am okay. Subject assumed. Nothing to say. I opened my phone and thought about typing: *I don't know how to answer a question like that.* But I didn't feel like responding and had told myself I wouldn't respond right away.

It felt good.

To watch the wing of the plane descend into cloud cover, luxurious as hotel soap, and not feel pained with the incessant desire to make things feel easy for another person.

An hour later, I got out of my seat and walked down the aisle toward the bathroom. I kept bumping into people's elbows and knees. I am constantly in the way. Or I feel constantly in the way. I feel an inability to control my body, to make it something not in the way. This is my problem with you: I am always in your way. My phone was in my hand, of course.

125

NUDES

Who's kidding who? I knew I would compose a text to you from the airplane bathroom. I felt sick the way I liked just thinking about it. Tiny beads of perspiration formed on my upper lip. I didn't wipe them away. I liked how awful you made me feel. I was never one to cut myself, for instance. I was a coward like that; I was selfish. I wanted you to do the cutting for me, figuratively speaking. And so far, you were happy to oblige. Asking if I was okay was just another cut. I slid the lock on the bathroom door and sat down on the toilet, staring at my phone, thinking about how best or worst to respond, like a good little masochist. I avoided the tiny airplane mirror. I avoided so much in my dedication to you. I avoided my bowels, which probably could have moved, had I been interested in them rather than in you. But of course I wasn't. My bowels were just another distraction, something else to ignore while I thought how best to respond to you, "my future, and my doom," as Cheever once wrote of his father.

You'd pulled back on me the night before.

We were supposed to meet in person for the first time, but my cabbie was late by fifteen minutes and when I'd showed up to the hotel, checked in, ran to the room breathless and slicked, my crisp collared shirt bleeding through with sweat, you were gone.

It was fifteen to midnight.

You had work the next morning, you'd said.

A life you had to return to,

a life that wasn't a fantasy.

I didn't think my way through my future the way you did.

I *felt* my way through it. Felt
Felt

     felt

          felt

              felt Like tiny hands through a wet orifice, searching for the foreign object. My fingers tapped my phone gently and satisfactorily then I patted my stomach like a tiny animal. There were two paths before me.

I could tell you the truth, that I wasn't okay, and had been sick with you for a very long time.	I could be the good girl. Pretend I, too, had a life like yours: filled with appointments, family gatherings, a career.

I turned the tap to hot and contemplated what it would take to smash the mirror to bits, to watch what remained of my wrist rinse away down the drain. Our final destination was two hours away; it was possible no one might find me until landing. Then what: I'd just be another news headline.

Why your cuts were so much more satisfactory: they kept me alive, feeding me piece by piece, threading me through my days.

I resolved then, to tell you how I felt.

I was hurt.

NUDES

I didn't understand how you could just leave me to myself like that.

I sent the message and a rush pooled at the top of my head. I sat down on the toilet, every bit of me relaxing. I slid open the door then

> panicked. None of it sent—a sign. You weren't really meant to know how I felt.

I wobbled back up the aisle, took my seat. I would be the good girl, then. Fate or destiny or the plane's crappy wifi had decided. I would fake my way through my life and yours, until I couldn't fake it anymore, then what? I would worry about that later. I was shaking and wishing for a scotch and soda but there was turbulence—in the air, also—and the pilot had made an announcement about the temporary suspension of services while I was in the bathroom. I considered hitting the button that would call a flight attendant, anyway. Would one of them have to come? Would they have to bring me a tiny bottle of scotch as per my request? If it were an emergency? If you had rebuffed me? Then I remembered I was going to be your good girl from now on and rested my hand in my lap with its partner. I gazed out the window remembering something you'd once told me about how little a person can survive on. At the time I took it as just another of your life wisdoms, something else you were teaching me, or trying to. Now, as the plane trembled and shook, I took it to be a warning for the future me, for the me on the plane. I must survive on so little, I thought. He is offering me so little and I am taking it.

Once on the ground, I considered carefully my options before locating a hardware store on the drive home. I bought a sledge hammer for $33. I wondered if it was the same brand Tom Brady used, Hillary Clinton.

The hammer's handle slid like sweating skin against my palm. Its weight was stable, comforting and balanced as I pulled it back above my shoulder, felt my centre of gravity shift, the striking muscles of my triceps and biceps engaging as I stopped its motion momentarily above my head. Then, I brought the hammer down.

My phone in shards.

I smashed my phone into nice, manageable pieces. Then I put the pieces in a freezer bag and smashed them some more until they became silvery, plastic shimmers.

I had decided to get a new phone and a new phone number. I had decided to be my own sadist and step one was disallowing myself to contact you. Step two was making myself a scotch and soda, smoking half a pack of cigarettes, ripping the filter off each before lighting it.

I could survive on so little—you were right. I was a survival-ist, now. I could give a TED Talk on surviving at some future date. I could write a how-to book on surviving. All I had to do was get through this one, endless night. I went online to see how late AT&T was open, if I could get there and get a new phone in time to text you before you went to bed. It'd been so long since we'd said goodnight. Two nights. Three nights, now.

NUDES

I didn't know if I could make it a fourth without my phone alighting with a text from you telling me I was your good girl. I didn't know if I would ever be able to sleep again without your goodnights. I lay down on my floor, filterless cigarette in mouth, to contemplate if I would be okay or not, if I would ever sleep again, if forty-five minutes was enough time to pull myself together and get to AT&T before they closed.

UNSOLVED MYSTERIES

HER HUSBAND REVEALED to her he'd been contemplating alternate versions of his suicide. She sat cross-legged on the floor, using the coffee table as an ironing board, preparing shirts for his new job. On the couch, the glow of the television on his glasses hid his eyes. The husband's voice was as gentle as a dinner conversation about the weather and her response was the same. She had spent time preparing for his death, hours imagining gruesome scenes of car accidents, urgently waiting for him to text or call whenever he'd made motorcycle trips. At night he fell asleep with the Colt 1911 under the bed, and she invented scenes of unfamiliar, armed men sneaking into the open windows of their small town apartment. When their fights got bad, she dreaded she would find him in the bathtub, bloody, teeth glistening like pomegranate seeds against the cracked, pale tile. This was the cost of falling in love with a man who had fought in two wars.

When they were dating, he'd always promised her that it was something he'd never go through with, for reasons of practicality:

NUDES

1. The mess. It would be too traumatic to leave something like that for her to clean up; he regarded her with a tender ferocity that he reserved only for livings things weaker than himself, such as small animals and young children.
2. It was common for the first suspect to be the spouse.
3. The world tended to blame women.

The iron hissed as she moved it algebraically across the shirt in clean triangles. It was worse now that she was pregnant, the fear of death. The death of what grew inside her, her death from car accidents or lightning strikes or tornadoes, the process of birth, her husband's ever-present potential abandonment, her inability to do anything that made more than minimum wage.

Linsey had spent the last decade cleaning the houses and hotels of the middle class. She was tormented by mothers who could afford both childcare and not to work whenever she cleaned the dust and grime from the corners of their kitchens, arranged the husbands' gifts of flowers to them on special days when the husbands were gone. The opened roses looked like screaming mouths.

Linsey envisioned the plight of being without a husband. Two days earlier, they'd watched old reruns of *Unsolved Mysteries*. The second episode talked about undelivered letters written by dead soldiers from World War II, how they'd finally made their way to the widows some forty years later. Linsey lay on her husband's shoulder, her head behind his field of vision. The widows, now senile and near infirm, had never remarried. Linsay's husband said it spoke to the character of the soldier. There was simply no one else that could be the same kind of man the soldier was, he said.

Before the job interview, he said he'd been planning routes far enough away from the houses she'd cleaned. He said it had to be far enough that it would guarantee an alibi for her in case the police made her a person of interest. It was petty, she thought, to consider suicide over things like employment or money or debt. It seemed more like an escape, into a world where those things had less weight.

"But they'd make you wait like three days before you could file a missing person's report," he said. "It all became too complicated."

Computer-generated soldiers made dying sounds on the television. Her expression was crisp and tightly restrained as she folded the arm of a shirt over, and began to smooth it out with the iron.

"Well, yeah," she replied. His rotting body made an appearance, danced between them like hail on the wet ground. She saw herself mourning in black, bemusing her new obsession with death. Her voice became soft and pithy, hoping to convey some sense that she understood but was not alarmed by his confession.

At least he was talking about it, a reassurance. And for now, the gun remained under the bed.

I LIVE IN A WORLD WHERE MEN WITH MONEY WANT TO TAKE AWAY MY WIFE

HE DOES ANGEL DUST in Brooklyn sex clubs, has a job that allows him to commute and fuck in the city. He has an array of stylish tattoos. I'm married, unemployed, afraid to eat toast. We are the same. All my boyfriends have been influencers, but I don't need the women I date to provide for me. Investing in people means eventually exploiting them.

Playboy was last active five hours ago. It's 3:32 a.m. I wonder if he's with E., which he probably is. I wonder if they've had sex before falling asleep. They are both fire signs. All fights in marriage come down to power. Of course, they've had sex.

Two weeks later I sit on the bed lotioning my legs, listening to the TV in the living room. E. is watching *Law and Order*. It's her favourite show. She's watched the series at least five times all the way through since we've been married. Olivia Benson murmurs on the screen, the season where they'd repeatedly found the bodies of small children hidden inside suitcases. Olivia Benson is the most unlikeable female character on TV. She says things that are flat, too hopeful. One of the bodies is a nine year old girl who's had a nose job, a beauty pageant contestant. You can't out-hope that. I lose myself in the slip of my hands greasing down my hairless skin, and imagine Playboy's mouth against E.'s knee, his bare teeth pulling gently at her patella. He looks up at her with his tired eyes, the whites grey with sleep.

She was his wife first. The fear of monogamy is that it ends— but E. had wanted it. The security. So badly she didn't want to compete anymore. I watched her give up her husband's six figure income to date a poet and become a sex worker in Berlin. That she could give some man a child and it wouldn't be enough terrified her. She had to trust the process and follow it through, believe by having a baby the man would see what she could do for him and how deep her commitment to securing his love could be. He was combative. But isn't every man?

I thought it was something. The day he flew into Tegel she went to see him. Every friend we had knew what he was, who he was, who his family was. They welcomed him anyway. I wondered what Mariska Hargitay would say. I didn't want to be like every other woman, sucking his dick in the hope that infamy planted itself inside them. He'd say he liked a thing (music, a hobby, a movie), and that made her want to try it more. One conflict crushes, opens another. Each word a silver tide swirling hooks through my sternum.

B.

*i want the first touch we have to be
our lips. to feel my hand against your neck,
then my mouth, then my teeth against the
fabric of your shirt*

E.

*i'd stoop down to unlace and remove
your shoes one by one, but i'd want you
looking at me the entire time.*

E.

*i'd want you to see the way i bite my
lip with each item of clothing i remove,
bc it means i'm getting closer to what
i want.*

B.

you can see the hunger in my eyes.

E.

a little shines.

E.

*i'd unbuckle the belt of your jeans
with my hands. the heat of my body
between your legs as i remove them,
run my hands up your thighs.*

B.

*once the barrier is broken, once i put
my mouth on you, there's really no going
back.*

NUDES

At night I can't sleep and in the morning I remember going through her phone again. I wake up groggy, and E. is tense. She wants me to be vulnerable but only in a language she can listen to.

E. and I take a trip around the city. The steering wheel hisses beneath her palms. The sky is more blue than I remember. I watch the sun blot shadows into the crepes of her skin. Stone monuments to the dead fence us in, and we circle, looking for a place to eat. I note an empty bank parking lot: she once got into his car here. I note an apartment complex: I'd seen the same car parked there, too. We turn right from a crossroads, and I see him walking down the street. My head pops off like a tire-pressure gauge. He is every man wearing a black t-shirt and designer jeans. He has money so there is no end to his wanting. E. pays for our lunch and I sulk in her impersonal conversation. My love for her is like the blunt side of an axe and with each pound I find new edges to the depths of my feelings.

E. feels a pain like yearning but doesn't show it. She can only love a person by betraying them. She is a lover I cannot have and think about all the time. All E. can think about is fucking her lover but instead she is fucking her wife. E. caresses her wife and says, "oh, yes," but she is saying it to her lover. Her wife pats her on the ass and E. smirks at her but E. is smirking at her lover. Her lover waits patiently for her inside her phone. Her lover is an unbroken thought. Her lover is an empty text box. And every day her wife interrupts each new one. She must violently flesh herself into every crevice of E.'s existence. She/I must remind her, constantly, of her/my presence. I guess this is just another one of those. One long, last beg. And all E. wants is one endless experience of what she loves. To exist in its flow, as one might stand beneath a waterfall. Neck broken by the weight of it.

POV

SUMMER THIGHS

I WANTED TO FUCK GOD or I wanted to fuck something else that wanted me on my knees. The pallor of his skin was all wrong. I tongued bite marks on the insides of my mouth, dry sockets sucking spit. Sweat dappled his cheeks. Light from the windshield on half his face. Hollow purple skin beneath his eyes. He pushed his hands against the girl in the backseat, unbuttoned her denim shorts. I watched from the front, his eyes with the nervousness of a dying race in a burning empire.

Sometimes I'd open my laptop just to watch me fuck myself. I wanted to know the things he did—I wanted to know about the anger, the DUI. I was curious how the therapist felt about him. I wondered what he told the therapist about my eyes. He thought they were green. I didn't feel the need to correct him. I could be a new person. Feel the hurt drop off like dead skin.

When you meet the person who made you like this and think

You're the reason I am like this

Before him, I was a small mammal with many teeth. After him, there were many things I didn't do because of fear. I was afraid of what someone might say or how they might treat me. I liked thinking about the time before because it was the last time I went after what I wanted. Everyone I'd ever been with loved me deeply. I guess I'd always been privileged in that way.

In the backseat, her body wrung out with anxiety, her feet made marks against the passenger window. He pushed her panties aside with his fingers, an infected scab on his middle knuckle, sucked her tongue into his mouth. Probably I was always waiting on men.

Body burned inside, a dry heat.

I turned around and looked away. Out the front windshield was field and moss, stone buildings in the distance, the sound of a train. I shouldn't have come here, for all the reasons I knew. I couldn't stay. It wasn't permanent. When the train first pulled in to the station, I walked until I came to the fascia of the building. The glow like a wasp in my vision. I saw them standing at the other side of the platform. I thought I could really end it in front of the train. There was a new wanting, a waning of what was possible but is no longer. I didn't want to be the kind of girl old men hit on, approachable to men who spent sad hours making bad paintings, expecting them to sell.

Before the station, I had watched the greenery pass from the train window and realised there may never be growth or change in E., and perhaps this permanent fixture of her misery is something that was made for me. This was not where I belonged. I could never leave her for all of the misery I felt, *her misery*, which I took inside my mouth and sucked the grit down until it was a hardened pearl. She had said once she was glad for this. That someone could see her pain. If we re-arranged the molecules and positioned ourselves in exactly the same place at exactly the same time at the very moment before our meeting, would we choose the same path? How you know fate is real, yes. That free will is a lie. Every molecule will do as every molecule does. You cannot change it. This was how I understood her.

We made eye contact. Me and the handsome man. The girl's feet were still at his shoulders, left foot on left shoulder, right on right. I had wanted to say beautiful but I didn't. I had reserved a word like beautiful for E. He was beautiful in a way that terror is beautiful. His hand at the back of my neck, his open fist covering my mouth. "How innocent," he said. There was that shine again ... I pulled out my phone, the camera lens a distraction. I pulled out my tongue, my longing for him a hot knife over an open wound.

There was that shine again. Again, there was that shine.

CHARLTON HESTON PLAYED JOHN THE BAPTIST BUT I REMEMBER HIM AS JESUS

ONCE, I was given a motorised ATV for toddlers. A photo of me exists somewhere standing on the ATV in pyjamas. I tried to drive it inside my small bedroom in Georgia, the whirring mechanical sounds of its cheap battery-powered engine, the plastic wheels scraping against a wooden door. I remember there was no room in the house for anything fun. I don't remember ever using it outside have recreated this memory from the photograph.

NUDES

It snowed when I was eight years old. This was the first time I remember seeing snow in Georgia. I made a chubby, short snowman with my uncle who was recovering from crack cocaine. The snow was not very good. It was wet and we had to scrape the whole front yard just to get enough for the snow-man. I may have reconstructed this memory from a photo also. I remember the sounds of my uncle's voice which seemed more childish than my father's. My father was a sergeant and so was always clean shaven. My uncle slept on our couch.

/

I'm in a bedroom, but I don't know where I am. I am not in Georgia. Maybe I am in my grandparents' house or maybe I am in the house we moved to in Colorado, but I was older when we moved and in this memory I am pretty young, six or eight years old. There is a lamp at the side of the bed. My dad is reading the Bible to me. He is talking about Jesus. The next day we will dress up and go to church and open presents when we come home. Twenty years later I live in Pentecostal coun-try and my mother is reminding me that I was baptised in the Methodist church. I ask my mom what being Methodist means and she says, "I don't know."

/

We only go to church that one time, or maybe we only go to church when we spend Christmas in upstate New York with my grandparents. The church is Baptist. My grandmother hands me a fiver for the tithe. I put the fiver in the big golden plate when it comes my way and notice how all the hymns are projected on big screen TVs. We take photos at breakfast after the service, the one time we all dress up nice. A church friend tells my parents that the soccer team has uniforms now, and I wonder how my grandmother can give us all money for the golden plate they pass around when neither her nor my grandfather has a job.

/

My father invents binge watching. In the days before Christmas we go to Blockbuster and Hollywood Video (both!) and he rents a series of movies, some based on a book series called *Left Behind* about a man and his daughter whose family disappears in the rapture, and some about the life of Jesus. Christmas Day is filled with TV sounds, first of the local parade, then the Charlton Heston movie *The Greatest Story Ever Told*, the one with Sidney Poitier, then of the apocalypse and rapture from *Left Behind*. We watch *Barabbas* and *King of Kings*. The TV is left on all day, my father watching in the living room while my mother cooks. In *Left Behind*, Kirk Cameron goes to the UN and accepts the word of God. I sit on one end of the couch and my dad sits on the other, a mountain of crumpled wrapping paper—opened gifts—between us. I don't have to read about Jesus in the Bible anymore.

/

My best friend and I drink cheap vodka in water bottles on Christmas Eve, watching Jesus movies with my parents. We are both eighteen, think we are smart enough to hide it and I'm unsure if my parents know and just let us drink, or if they really can't tell.

NUDES

/

Waiting on Christmas dinner because my dad is working. My dad is working all the time. Counting my calories then counting my prayers then counting my blessings.

/

Waiting for my dad to visit, spending Christmas in upstate New York with my grandparents and my mother. One of my last vivid memories of them. I think I am sixteen or seventeen. I contemplate throwing up the Christmas dinner contents of my stomach in the hallway bathroom but the house is old, the walls are thin, and the plumbing may not hold.

/

Drinking with my parents on Christmas Eve. Making Christmas dinner because my mom is working. The sounds of the parade on TV, then maybe football, then Charlton Heston, again, always.

/

Things I don't remember:
- most of my presents
- family dinners
- the amount of times my dad or mom was working on Christmas or Thanksgiving
- when or why we stopped going to my grandparents' for holidays

- when I started drinking on Christmas Eve
- the night I drank the entire contents of my parents' fridge when I was twenty-one and my mom found out Christmas morning because I didn't go to bed until sunrise (I do remember a couple cases of Guinness, plates of deviled eggs, pigs in a blanket, condiments, pastel Tupperware containers of vegetables pre-prepped for Christmas day; I don't remember what the sun
- looked like as it rose, I don't remember falling asleep on the couch as Mom came downstairs for coffee, the first awake, as always. I do remember the black garbage bag filled with empty bottles that she carried to the garage).
- how old I was when she told me "you're just like your father" as a form of punishment and the shame I felt
- when I switched from regular Coke to Diet Coke
- when I switched from beer to liquor
- why my uncle stopped coming around to hang out
- when we stopped watching Jesus movies
- why we stopped photographing our moments together, when everything good is so easily forgotten.

RIFLE

THIS SUMMER, Luis sent a series of postcards from Vegas, Disney World, and Los Angeles. The last one said he was moving back home. Here, to the place we grew up. He'd been gone five years. I'd never left this town. Once, we went to a big city on the front range for my mother's birthday; once we went to Gunnison to fish for carp. It was all the same high mountain desert, brittle brush on the side of the road, red clay cuddling yucca. In his card, he said he'd lost his job, needed to find home base again, a place to recover. The blue ink dipped and rose like valleys in a mountain range and said: *Rifle is cheap and quiet.* It said, *I've also missed you, so there's that.*

/

The summer after we graduated, my father got fired from his job on one of the farms. I worked the register at the general store to help out. Luis told me he would stay the summer and after that, he would be gone. He wanted to be a famous photographer, he'd said, and couldn't do it by staying here.

NUDES

I had this six-foot antique hookah sitting in my room and told Luis I needed his help to turn it into a lamp. I was constantly using ploys like this to get him to come over. He seemed captivated with me when I was around, but when he wasn't near me I was forever wondering how he felt.

When I told him about the hookah, he laughed. I rubbed the soft bronze with my hands. My fingers traced divots where pentacles were carved into the metal, blackened from years of dirt. I never finished projects and he knew it. Sometimes you need to force things.

"If we make it a lamp, we could have three wishes," he said.

I couldn't run the cord through the stem of the hookah, so instead of making a lamp, I filled it with water until it overflowed, cleaning out the insides. Luis made tar tobacco with rose petal molasses and thick, sweet honey. This became our ritual. With a lump of coal on top, we'd suck the sweet sugar smoke into our lungs, releasing the billows like tiny trains.

The day before he was going to leave, I bought a dozen bouquets. My bedroom filled with the thick, peaty smell of lilacs and lavenders, roses and sweet alyssum; I hung garlands of gardenias around the garden level windows. Luis sat on my bed, muddling together that tar tobacco in a bowl. I was half-sarcastic about the lamp. Who'd ever wished on a light bulb and an electric cord?

He took a break from the rose and honey mixture and scratched his beard, which had grown in thick over the spring.

"Why is it always three wishes, anyway?" I asked.

He picked up a spoon and fed the tobacco mess into the bowl, big as my fist, then placed the aluminum on top.

"Three is a magic number," he said. "One is the beginning.

Two is the struggle. Three is progress. Evolution. That's what I want."

He poked holes into the aluminum. Then he lit the coal, placed it on top, replaced the cover. His ceremony. He sat down on the floor, sucking in air from the hose. I wanted growth, too. Or movement. For him, that meant travel. He wanted to forget Rifle, see the vast belly the country had to offer. My parents needed me, and besides, I couldn't think of anything else I would do. I didn't know anything else. I sat next to him on the floor and pushed my fingers into the blue plush plumes of carpet. I closed my eyes and my fingers and palms turned into roots and my hair began sprouting leaves. I didn't want him to leave. My skin crackled into the grey ash of aspen bark when his voice broke my transformation.

"What would you want?" I heaved my chest.

"I don't know," I said.

My father grew more miserable each day and my mother made dinner every night like things would be okay. We did not discuss troubles out in the open but when I was alone with her, in hushed tones, she told me we were falling behind on the mortgage. I needed to keep working to help the family out, she said. I thought of the general store, the moldy smell of the building, the measly paycheck. But the owner, Jim, said he'd increase my hours, so it looked promising.

I sank into the pillows on the couch, throwing my hands behind my head. Luis's body felt warm next to mine and I did not want that to change. I didn't want anything to change.

"I want to freeze time," I said.

He laughed in this way, a sort of half-giggle that caught his chest. I didn't think that freezing time was as farfetched as evolution.

"The past is still a part of you," he said. "But you can't stop progress."

I cradled his fingers against my palm and placed his hand on my thigh. I let it rest there as we sat, staring at the garlands on the windows. The light cast shadows of flowers against our skin.

It didn't matter what we did, or if he felt anything for me, as long as the moment could be remembered.

"What would your second wish be?" I asked. He pulled me closer to him, smiled softly. then let his eyes wander toward the window.

That night his body was heavy against mine. I put my hand over his mouth, urging him to be quiet.

Afterward, we drank wine from my mother's stash and took turns taking photographs of each other in the mirrors on my closet doors with his camera. The flash washed us out. It darkened the reflections with bright stars in the middle of the photographs where we stood holding the camera. We looked like other-worldly angels, fairy creatures. Like each picture caught all the light inside of us. He asked me to pose, and we made it a game.

"Move your head this way," he said, then, "adjust your shoulder here." I sprawled on my bed, messing up my childhood sheets prints of Russian bears in ballerina costumes. I unbuttoned my cutoff shorts. He posed my hands across my topless body, snapped the photos, and looked at each shot on the LCD screen.

"Half of performance is the show," he said.

"What's the other half?" I scowled, pretending I was intimidating. I tried to squint my eyes and pout my lips. I was always trying to be cool. I think he knew that.

From the balcony of my parents' home, we watched the sun rise over the Roan Plateau. My parents would be awake soon;

I had to shoo him out before they knew he'd spent the night. He'd be leaving in a few hours, to New Mexico, maybe, a busier place. There were only a few moments I remembered—short, intense bursts of light triggered by certain smells or colours. Like a photograph stuck in a box somewhere and relived later.

/

The last image in my mind is like this: Luis stands in my doorway, slim flanneled shoulders against the door jamb. My arms inside his jacket. Words inside every other kiss, he's saying, *Come with me, come with me, come with me.* But I can't do that. He says I have these real doe eyes, the way I look at him like a young Jean Harlow, my round face.

The way this scene ends, I stare at him through the crack in my door, wind blowing onto my face. I let us die in the spot in my doorway. I can't cry.

/

When Luis moved back, it felt like time travel. Like we were meeting for the second first time, resurrecting reincarnated lives.

I had been a different person the last five years. My parents were renting a place a couple streets away. There was no need to pretend everything was normal anymore. My father was free to drink, it was as good excuse as any to sink further. The owner of the general store had promoted me to manager—a banal sense of purpose in my life. There had been other men. The tattoo artist. The gas station attendant. The plumber's son. They were just a bunch of dumb something elses. No one felt important or permanent or serious.

When Luis moved back, he brought a girlfriend. There was no mention of this, of her, in his postcards, nowhere at all did he say——. I was stocking canned pumpkin, canned corn, canned cherry pie in aisle three when I heard a cough and he was there holding two bottles of water and a bag of trail mix. I rang him up and asked if he was free that night.

"My girlfriend," he said. "She's waiting in the car."

Past midnight, I got a text: *I want to see you, so there's that.*

It wasn't the same. Each awkward smile, my dry mouth when he looked at me this certain way. Like he wanted me to bite his lip, wrap my arms around his neck and squeeze. Then he'd leave. "Gotta be back at nine o'clock." My stomach burned, empty and hot.

I wanted to go to an art gallery one night. A friend at work was having a show and I wanted Luis to come, too. I drove us up the road to Silt, a smaller town just east. The gallery was in a homesteader's cabin, about a hundred years old. In my rusted eighties sports car, we pulled up the gravel drive and this tiny house stood underneath an umbrella of Chinese elms. Apricot, apple, and plum trees surrounded the fieldstone building. The art itself wasn't much. It was dark when we left.

When we parked at my apartment building, he hugged me goodbye and hesitated a second before letting go. Almost two months to the day of his arrival back, after keeping my distance for so long, this was the moment he chose to stop moving. I leaned into him, quickly reaching for the door handle on his side and pushed him out of the door, out into the cold, leaning into the passenger seat. I tucked my chin a bit and raised my eyes at him in that Jean Harlow way he liked so much.

"Get outta here," I said. "You're killing me, man."

He smirked, working over the drama between us.

"You're going to make me walk home?" he said with an uncertain laugh. He wrapped his arms around his sides, rubbed the flannel shirt he was wearing. "It's so cold."

I held my breath so long, trying to decide the right course of action. I saw spots in my vision. I heard him kick the gravel a bit, move his feet.

I said, "Okay."

I said, "Get in, I'll drive you home."

His fingers rubbed cautiously against the fabric between my thighs. I rocked my hips against his hands as his mouth pushed against mine, teeth and tongue. He shivered so I placed my palms beneath his shirt, caressing the warmest parts of him.

After that, Luis walked the half-mile home. *I have to go*, he said, over and over again, murmurs in my mouth. Home to the place he lived with his girlfriend. I was sleepless that night, and for many nights after.

Desperate to get him to come over, I became obsessed with those things I could not have. It was the same game. Was he thinking of me? I would text or call and get no answer for hours, a day or two. It was as if he did not understand the urgency of the situation, of my need to be together in the same place.

He left for an assignment, told me he'd come back a day early so we could spend the night together. I counted the minutes until his arrival and cooked peppered beef tips in local butter, pan-fried summer squash fritters, baked a thick rhubarb pie for dessert. Pretending, the way my mother did, that it wasn't all going to end.

We drank cheap beer after beer, hardly touched the squash or the pie. When it was dark, I grabbed a blanket big enough to wrap around us and took him out to my balcony. I had only a downstairs neighbour. No cars were passing through. At midnight you heard crickets, maybe an owl. We lay in the blanket, our hot breath beneath it, and looked up at the star sea above us.

"It's not like this in cities, you know."

I laughed and shifted against him, our shoulders touching.

"I know, silly," I said. "I know there's a world outside of this town."

"You might know," he said. "But you've never seen it."

A hint of resentment thronged my body. I'd never be as traveled as his girlfriend. I didn't even know what she looked like—I imagined tall, beautiful, bland and tan. I rolled my head against him, pushed my face hard against his shirt. He was right. I'd been here so long I was afraid to leave.

Underneath the blanket, I pushed myself on top of him, our hips touching. His hands formed a gentle circle around my neck as I tugged his pants off, and then mine, moving my panties aside.

When his girlfriend found out about me, she left back to wherever it was they met. Somewhere in the heat of Albuquerque. I was singing to heartbreak songs on my way to work one day when I realised she might be singing the same song to herself on the same highway, thinking about me.

After the breakup, he avoided me for weeks. My suddenly free schedule consisted of getting drunk alone on hibiscus-infused vodka and rosewater tea, playing Cat Stevens over and over again on my laptop while I cried on my couch. I blamed myself. Sometimes I'd just sit on the floor and use my coffee table as a prop for my head. Rolling into work the next day with braided unwashed hair, crumpled clothes.

It was after this Luis came to me one night, knocking hard. I opened the door a crack, the chain still on.

"Come west with me," he said. "I'm leaving."

I hadn't seen him in three weeks. He wanted to live in Vegas where I imagine the air has that electric quality when it storms and the lights make you dizzy. Where the city glows like glass in the sand.

"Don't you want a bigger life?" he asked.

A bigger life. The wasteland air snap of a hot dust bowl. I wasn't sure what to say so what I did was stare at him, stare past him, at the darkness of the sky around him.

I undid the chain and led him inside, then I sat at the plastic dining room card table. Cheap lawn furniture, two small cushioned chairs, one cradling me. To my back was an open window, breeze coming in. It was a cool night, but mild. Warm enough for the mosquitoes.

"Look, my lease is up."

I lit a cigarette, focused my eyes on the flame. "Already?"

His car was packed with everything he'd ever owned, he said. A few posters and plastic cups, a record player, an air mattress.

"Are you coming with me?"

I looked beyond him, into the night. Across the street was a row of tiny homes, all neighbours I knew, people who held the place up with their feeble fingers, people who chose to stay during hard winters, during bad financial times, who had never known to choose anything different than the life they had now. Luis was someone who would stop choosing me.

I had prayed for him to come home and once he did, I stopped praying.

My head buzzed hot, my limbs turned pink with the fear of truth-telling. I explained how I had to pay off some bills before

I could move. My parents still needed me, they'd need to find a replacement at the general store. I said I'd follow him out there after a few months, but it wasn't the truth. The truth stayed inside, burning me up. I could not say no to something I'd wanted for so long, which now became something I feared. Not outright. The buzzing inside me grew with every word, and then I swear it bounced across the room. I sucked air through my teeth, let it out slowly through my nose. We only existed in the looks we gave each other, across dinner tables, in art galleries, holding hands. I knew this now.

I told him I loved him, he could go and I would follow. Then a buzz came from the ceiling. Like it had leaked out of my head and flew frantically around. It hit the light bulbs with a little pink, pink, pink.

Memory made me relive the way we fell in love, over and over again. It was just legend. The pink pink sound. My head buzzing above. Just said yes to say no later. I thought back to hanging gardenias on the windows, our Friday nights when we'd smoke rose tobacco and make up wishes. The way a person sticks to you. You have to slough off the skin.

"Before you go," I said. "Tell me about your third wish." I waited to see if he remembered. Couldn't read if he knew I was lying this whole time or if he was just quiet until finally— "Wasp," he said. What?

"Wasp," he said. "Wasp!"

Luis ran into the living room as I looked up, and there it was, flying around, looking for any way out. I tore open the kitchen cabinets underneath the sink and grabbed a bottle of blue window cleaner, holding it like a gun. My eyes darted around the dining room and kitchen. Luis peeked around the corner.

It's graceful, the way a wasp flies. They look like little fairies when the light reflects right, wings like gossamer, dainty legs. I waited for it to land. Its legs touched the countertop and it stopped. Luis' eyes were wide like he'd never been stung. I cocked the cleaner gun and shot—squirts of blue liquid coated the insect and it fell to the floor.

In a puddle, this dangerous little beast was harmless. I got on my hands and knees and stared, as close as I could get, watching the wings struggle to beat in the liquid. Luis watched me watching it. The wasp seized, curled up and uncurled until finally, it stopped moving.

"Hey," Luis said. "I really have to go."

He grabbed me around the waist to hug me, my hand with wet paper against my chest. It bled through on both our shirts as our bodies came together.

It was at least eight hours to Vegas. He had a long night ahead of him. "I know," I said. I kissed him in that movie star way, leaning against the doorjamb, a holy spot. I watched him walk down the stairs as I closed the door, still clutching the wet ball of paper and the wasp.

SNUFF

SNUFF

DEATHWISH 006

AT LEAST ONCE A WEEK, I walk to and from the liquor store, thinking about if I'll die on the way there. I hold the neck of the glass bottle in a way that makes it easy to swing at someone's face. I look both ways three times before crossing and imagine a car that comes out of nowhere. I can almost feel the impact, liquor and purse and teeth flying into the air the way I have seen in all those videos on LiveLeaks. My fiancé says he stands at our 5th floor balcony, watching me walk home.

When I fight with him I wonder if I'll die in the dark corner of our bathroom, fileting myself with his straight razor. Disembowel the parts of me that need to lie empty like the space in bed between us, as much distance between his body and the wrongs in mine as possible. I lie with my back to him in the dark, curl fingers into fists. On rainy days, when I turn left, go over 55 mph, I think if I'll die while driving. When he puts his feet up on the dashboard I see his ex-wife's calves there, the smooth curve of what they were before the accident. There are ways of being broken that feel like a kind of death. A car pulls out in front of us and he gasps and pulls his feet down quick. Adidas shoe prints left oily on the windshield. I imagine those calves, the exposed bone he described. The gaping skin and meat, how I learned what "compound fracture" means. He says he can't look at my legs, ever.

GLOCKJAW

THE NURSES WILL NOT let me watch TV. They say the stress could impede my ability to heal. I touch my jawline where gauzy bandages wrap around my head, and below that, find a long, sickle-shaped wound in my abdomen, sucking skin and blood clots (I peeked underneath it and was scolded when the bandage would not re-adhere). A numb but broken leg is held in a swing.

Thoughts disappear into the ether. They come and go and I cannot catch them. I want to tell them to you, flits of images, phrases that seem important, some secret that must be revealed, but something stops them. It begs at my ankles, rips at my clothes every time I try to put it down.

I wait for someone to come see me—a husband, a sister, a friend, but I hear so much madness in the hospital I start to wonder if they might be bedridden, too (or worse, if I am alone. If I have always been alone).

The nurses say my name is Amanda but I feel more like an Angel. The last thing I remember: white fluorescent light of a women's bathroom. Then something large, expanding like a sound; I became unsure of my footing and dizzy, realised the floor itself was swaying. I think I'd made it to the tenth floor by then. I ran towards the heavy bathroom door, pressed against it, ears ringing. The air pushed out of my lungs as if they were little Ziplock bags. As the door opened, a tremendous and terrifying light. Pulsating from white to yellow to blue over and over again until there was no colour at all, only an absence.

Three different nurses visit me: one in the morning, one in the afternoon, and one at night. I want them to stay and talk to me but they won't. They are always leaving. A name and some code called to different floors every few minutes.

The blonde one enters so I know it is afternoon. I struggle to remember her name, even though I see her daily. I ask her about the news. Any movement feels as though the skin around my jaw might rip apart. The nurse refuses to look at me, puts a curl of hair behind her ear. Red veins irrigate the whites of her eyes. I want to know what happened, I say. She pours a clear solution into the wound on my abdomen, replaces the sheets, redresses the wound. I get angry and then cough from my anger, every muscle engaging in my core. It is the worst pain I have known and the days rotate around this pain like a tumbling gem, each moment revealing a new face. On the tabletop beside the camera is also a cell phone and a dusty wallet. It coats my fingers, forming cracks in the skin. There is not much there: my name on a driver's license, a photo. Brunette hair cropped to chin, thin lips. My name is Amanda Carhartt. I live at 375 Hudson, apartment number four. I weigh a hundred and twenty pounds and I am five-six and I have hazel eyes.

I touch the stitches on my jaw and the nurses slap my hands away, telling me it will get infected. They re-bandage the wound but I continue to pull it off. I press the power button on the camera, and the screen flashes blue before coming alive. I point it at my body, white sheets, corpse-looking bruises across my midsection. I take a picture and it flashes bright and reminds me of leaving the bathroom—the opening door, the intense heat, the feeling of nothing. My heart races. I turn off the flash, turn the camera towards my face, take another picture. It is too dark to see anything: the outline of a face, the whites of eyes.

I try to turn on the cell phone but it is dead and I throw it across the room. The burnt smell never abates. It is the smell of melted plastic, charred hair, of a roast that has been in the oven too long.

My hunger returns and I eat cup upon cup of vanilla pudding and then shit myself in my sleep. Too embarrassed to call for help, I wait until Morning Nurse comes, like an infant let the pressure of her hands clean me down there with something cold and wet, and her slim fingers apply a cream, she places a pad beneath me, she washes her hands in the adjoining bathroom. I apologise to her and then I begin to cry. I ask her when I can leave. I pull at her clothes, try to tell her about the thoughts that keep disappearing, that something is missing in me. It's okay, she says. It's going to be okay. She puts a hand on my head and I know she is lying. I become aware of a new bandage on my scalp, I feel her fingers touch a bald patch.

When she leaves, I stroke my fingers across the suede feeling of new hair growth across my head. I pick up the camera again and consider turning on the flash but my chest becomes tight and I wheeze. Night Nurse will be here any minute and I want to see myself before she arrives. I turn it on and my hands shake and I drop the camera. Then I pick it back up. Sweat forms on my chest. I lick my lips, taste salt. I point the camera at my face, try to smile. A stitch pulls, or something pops—a rip. The flash hits my eyes, yellow then orange then complete black—everything darker than it was before. In the flash, wind whips across my face, water streaks from my eyes, the hoarseness hits my throat.

I scroll back through the pictures on the camera. The first of my face. I see the girl from the driver's license but it is not the same girl. She looks old. The stitches along her cheek make the shape of a glock. Evening Nurse said my jaw broke into sixteen pieces. I tongue the space inside my mouth, sharp and tasteless inside, empty sockets in the gum, like pulsing cotton.

The picture before that is the one of my body, the white, formless shapes and shadows of the sheets.

The picture before that is of a bathroom—fluorescent lights. There is Amanda reflected in the mirror, there is the camera, there is the cell phone in her front jean pocket, there is a lanyard around her neck with a tag on it.

Then a photo of an office building in flames, a photo of a man running towards the camera with blood on his hands, his cheeks, his eyes far away, somewhere else.

The geometric shapes of a stairway full of smoke. More bloodied people in the lobby of a building, walking, looking around.

The photos lead out of the building onto the street which is covered in what looks like snow, a photo panned upward toward a silver skyscraper crowned with smoke, then down the street; I flip through them, more people running. A single building on fire, until the last: pale yellow, the silhouette of a woman in a pencil skirt, hair in a bun. She is wearing a pearl necklace, gold earrings. You cannot see the colour of her clothing. She looks at me, her mouth gaping, eyes bulged, three inches of dust. And her hands, they are reaching. She is reaching for me.

SATANISM

IN SPRING, BIRDS COME. Unmown grass fruits seeds. A small indent in the weeds shivers as something moves through it, like someone lost in a corn maze. I approach the bird but like most sick animals it runs from help. I crawl towards it, my shoulder blades pulsing beneath my thin-strapped tank top. Ivan steps out of the house in khakis and a long-sleeved collared shirt with a red name tag. His shiny leather shoe pushes grass apart. Soil bleaches cold into my kneecaps. The bird hops again.

Ivan bends down and picks up the bird, its red breast beating. I look at it, thinking it looks like a feathered heart. But I know a bird is not a heart. A heart does not belong in a pair of hands.

It's a robin chick, says Ivan. He splays one wing out to show holes where feathers should be, empty tooth sockets.

I think he knows everything about animals like a Boy Scout or farmer. Ivan grew up on mountainsides, was deployed to resorts and deserts. Places he was meant to die. Now he works security for armored trucks. Ivan lived many different lives before me and I am interested in all of them.

NUDES

I get off my knees, go into the house. My eyes feel like burnt light bulbs screwed into their sockets, draining energy yet not working. The dog jumps in excitement and his paw scratches my arm. The dog hurts because he loves. He doesn't know what hurt is when done out of love. I step back outside, stand with the shoebox next to Ivan, waiting. We'd adopted the dog to prove our commitment to each other exactly one year ago, and had made the decision to adopt again, this time my sister's baby. My mother had called, pleading, for me to take the baby. I think of my sister's life, sitting in cars inhaling black smoke from aluminum foil through pen tubes. My sister's dry cough, my sister's body limp in the bathroom doorway, legs kicked out into the hall.

Ivan looks at my arm, the scratch joining dozens of ropey self-inflicted scars. Ivan makes a disapproving sound. He asks if anyone will adopt the dog.

I shake my head no, lying.

Ivan and I lie in bed scrolling through news, the dog at our feet. There is never anything of significance to discuss. The world will go on hurting just the same. I turn to him, admiring how the dim light makes his teeth look like little tombstones. I look at Ivan because I am anticipating. I've been taught to do this all my life.

Greg has taken dogs out to the woods before, he says.

Who is Greg, again? I ask.

Works on finance side, Ivan says. Greg said taking dogs out to the woods is awful. Greg said, you don't want death on your conscience. But Greg forgets who I am, says Ivan.

I recall the history of Ivan-in-Uniform, Ivan-with-Crew-Cut. Memory spreads like blood through gauze.

Have you killed dogs before, I ask. I had always assumed Ivan's killed other men. It was easy to think of those deaths as an abstraction. The dog seems so human when his little eyebrows move this way and that.

Tons, says Ivan. None of them made me feel like that. I imagine the dogs. Stray dogs in the desert; no names or collars. At the edge of our bed, our dog shivers, his collar twinkles. He looks up.

Why do men kill, I ask.

Because women ate the apple, Ivan says sarcastically. I don't laugh at the joke. He looks at his phone for a second, then back at me.

The fruit was offered out of love, I say. It was the workshop of the self.

Ivan sighs. I try to think of some consolation to give about Greg but the scratch on my wrist busies my mind. I put my hand on his shoulder and squeeze. His eyes are grey, muddled by humidity and beer. I give the only consolation I can provide. I lean in to part his lips; I use my tongue.

Ivan presses his fingers into my pinkest parts. I imagine the feel of my insides, his fingers rough. Ivan's thumb, placed gently on my pulsing little bump, moves one way then another. The soft light changes red to pale on the curves of our skin. Ivan puts one hand on my chin, pushes my lip into my bottom row of teeth with his thumb until the membrane splits. I like to be cut like this. Ivan is pumping. Ivan is a machine and I'm a carcass on a conveyer belt. Metallic spit works its way through my gums. I let his slide take me. For a moment, I see myself from above. My face round, chin tucked into my neck. Eyelids loose, the whites look ecclesiastical. Our bodies split, wetness seeping from between us.

NUDES

Ivan wipes water from his lips, puts his head back. Look at me, I say.

Ivan doesn't look. What do you hope to achieve, he says. I wonder, too. Lately everything feels inconsequential. Experiences fall through me like a sieve. I consider accepting custody of my sister's baby. I consider abandoning the dog. There isn't any judgment but there isn't anything else, either.

Ivan and I are quiet while he waits for an answer. Ivan says his father stared at him every day as a boy.

Ivan says, Intimidation.

People project feelings onto other people, I say.

I feel split open. Like a hand hammered against pavement, peach skin meshed out red into asphalt grooves. The pulse of blood moves beneath the stretch of his fingers, over my hip.

Ivan goes to the bathroom to get water. The medicine cabinet opens, a plastic lid pops. A pill is crushed against the counter.

It's discipline, he says. To stare and be stared at.

It's not about not blinking, I say. My voice goes high and tight. Ivan bends over and sniffs something off the counter. He stands up and moves into the doorway, half in and half out of the light.

What are we doing about the dog, he asks. He sniffs again, shorter, touches his nose with a finger, comes back to bed. His body loosens, eyes close, his tongue and jaw go slack. I slink from the bed and head into the bathroom, pull half-blades from a yellow box on his side of the bathroom cabinet, thinking about what I want. What I want is natural. What is natural is what I want. The tile is cold against my bony ass. The blade is thin as paper. It separates the skin. The gutter in my leg opens white then slowly fills with blood.

The next day I'm on a highway when the fresh remains of an animal split traffic. The back half of a deer, or maybe a large, tan dog, tall enough to hit a bumper, is spread out over the middle lane. Everything pink inside. I count three legs. I think of my sister. She was hit last summer crossing a country highway at night. What were the odds, I think, when you could see headlights coming. I imagine her body in five pieces among the shoulder gravel.

I turn onto my home street and see specks of blood on the windshield, hit the lever to spritz. The wipers move but the blood stays, a neon red drip. At home, the shoebox on the patio is empty. Across the yard something parts the grass in little thumps and I'm there again, knees wet. The little bird gulps air. One eye closes, the membrane thin and bunching up along the eyelid. I claw at dirt until I find an earthworm.

The bird's mouth opens and I push the worm in, but it doesn't take. Then the bird doesn't open its mouth anymore.

I am tired. I think about cataloguing all the days I feel like dying. But then I think Ivan would find the death catalog. Ivan would use it against me. I have no reason to think he would, but still it occurs to me. I make an enemy of men because I am afraid. I try to correct my thinking, but I also want to close my eyes and lie down like the bird. A large hand presses into my shoulder. I turn around and see Ivan against the cold grey sky, clouds papered above. Ivan leans into me, breathing against my neck.

I could crush it, he says. The heat of his breath gives his words a torpid colour.

I shake my head. He puts his fingers in my hair like a comb and pulls them out halfway, then rests his palm on the back of my neck. It feels heavy. I am newly surprised by his strength.

It's bleeding, I say. I hear my own voice inside more than outside, stumble along the hard sounds in *bleeding*. I walk around

NUDES

the yard in platform sandals, making wide steps to avoid dew on the grass. My feet get wet anyway. I pick up twigs, blades of grass, another worm, and bring them all to the bird. Flies buzz around, landing on its open eye.

Even the flies know what's coming, Ivan says. When I look up, it's all clouds.

Just throw it over the fence, he says. I shut my eyes, an outline of Ivan and the bird and the dog and the backyard, hot and beating.

My sister had been hitchhiking with her boyfriend, backpacking through national forests. She was enjoying a wild freedom, the kind I pretended to enjoy when I went into the backyard to sit under trees. Eventually, the bugs would bite, air would cake my make-up. I'd rush back inside, sliding the door, the cool velvet of the couch against my itching legs. I pick up the bird and walk to the back of the yard, a wild alleyway of unmanaged weeds. I think of my sister on the road, looking down at her thighs, at the asphalt. Or maybe she looked up, head thick with wishes, eyes wide at the red wash of light on her lover's face. I cradle the bird with both hands and split them open over the fence, watching as it disappears into brush. It falls like a fat apple. I wait to hear the impact.

ROOM SERVICE

ON OUR WEDDING NIGHT David shows me what it takes to kill a man. In the hotel room, we lie on the unmade California king, my stockings slick against the stainless white sheets. David opens his laptop and navigates to a website full of recordings like this: a video of a man being burnt alive in a cage, his body going taut and black; a video of a man getting shot in the head, a cavity the size of a fist blowing out the back of his skull. There are a lot of things I don't know about my new husband. He looks at me when he pulls up the video. His eyes are sallow and set back like a farm animal, expressive and docile.

I pretend to watch, but I focus my eyes on the intricate beading of my wedding dress draped over a chair in the corner. My breasts ache. A man on the screen shrieks and a sheet of goosebumps appears on my skin. I am filled with something soft and new and want to cry, but nothing comes. I imagine the funeral, open casket, the man's head sewed shut where the bullet left, sunken in like a newborn's fontanelle.

Once, my sister asked me to watch her baby. I'd never been around a baby before. I put the baby on the bed to change its diaper and turned around for a second. The cold thud of its body against the hardwood paralysed me. I waited for it to scream or cry. Before I turned around, in that split second of silence, I imagined the baby was dead, how my sister would never forgive me and forever be marred by its absence. But the baby wasn't dead. The baby just sat there. I looked at the baby and the baby looked at me.

First the baby said *Mamamamamamama*

Then the baby said *Dadadadadadadada*

Then the baby said *A-dah, a-dah, a-dah, UGH, se-se-se-se-se-se-se-se-se*

I stood there, watching language form in the mouth of the baby. How a syllable was connected to each emotion, the da connected to the loud emotions and the ma connected to the quiet emotions. When the baby tried to move its lumpy body, it kicked its legs hard in the air and the baby banged its head and nothing happened.

In our hotel room, David takes off his black trousers and his shiny new shoes and puts them directly on top of my dress. I don't say anything about the shoes on the dress because I bought it from a Salvation Army for less than twenty dollars, and there were already yellow armpit stains in the lace and brown spots on the train.

He gets into bed with me, puts his hand into a bag of potato chips. He eats the chips one by one, wiping crumbs onto the comforter before navigating to another video on his laptop.

"Movies make death sterile," he says. "There is a lot more blood in violence than you think."

I sip champagne from a plastic flute while the video plays. It's from a series called "Cops versus the Public." Sometimes the public wins, but mostly the cops do. In one, a man in Los

Angeles is being commanded to release his gun as he stands on his doorstep, four flashlights pointed at him, four cops behind the camera. The man hesitates, then throws the weapon, underhanded, to the ground. Someone releases a K9 unit. As the German Shepherd rushes towards the man, one cop fires, and then everyone fires.

The cops empty their clips into the man and the dog. David says, "Fuck L.A."

"Why?" I ask.

I ask my new husband a lot of questions.

David says the cops in L.A. are always ready to fire. That he once had a gun pulled on him for a routine traffic stop.

"What were you doing in L.A.?"

The receding edges of his mouth tremble. "Nothing," he says. "I was traveling out there to buy a car."

He unbuttons his shirt and removes it and I rub my hands across his back, feeling the raised scars of the blackand-white chainlink fence tattooed across his shoulder blades. There are three letters in the tattoo, abbreviations or initials. He won't tell me what they mean.

Three weeks ago, I offered him a place to stay when we met in line at CVS. I was filling a prescription for Ativan and he was buying Bronkaid and caffeine tablets. Something about the shape of his body told me he'd done terrible things. I had always wanted to date a man I thought might murder me.

The hotel is the nicest place I've ever slept and as I move my legs across the sheets I know I am not good enough for them. I don't ask David how much the room cost or how he paid for it. He lights a cigarette and I take another sip of champagne and ask him for a cigarette. He hands me the one he just started, flipping it around the way you hand someone a sharp knife, butt end first. I take the cigarette and then he lights his own. I watch him wipe potato grease off his fingers onto the perfect white sheets before touching the keys on his laptop.

The champagne bottle is almost empty. I ask my husband if it's okay to call room service for another and he says, "Yes, baby, but we have to put the cigarettes out first."

I grab a pillow from the bed and hold it across my breasts. "Why do they empty the entire clip?" I ask. My husband says something about 9 mm bullets and how they are useless. He puts a large hand on my stomach and rewinds the video of the man in L.A. He plays it again, frame by frame.

Here is where the man releases the gun, here is when the gun is five inches away from his hand, when a cop releases the German Shepard, when a cop shoots first. Here is when everyone else fires, and then the man goes down and kicks his legs into the air; and here it's too dark to see what the dog is doing but we know the dog is dead. David says, "Do you see how it takes a firing squad? It lets everyone feel like they've killed while absolving them of knowing who did it, who had the confirmed kill." When I take too many pills, a sinking feeling envelopes me. When I lie down I go deeper than my bed. I lie into the floor, beneath the floor, and feel smothered. But the smothering isn't claustrophobic. It feels comforting, like a womb.

"Do you think they can feel their life leaving?" I ask.

He moves his hand to my chest, grabs my tit, swollen like a nectarine. "The brain goes on repeat," he says. "Shock pushes the body to move so even while it's dying, it doesn't know it's dying." He massages his thumb in circles in a way that hurts and I don't say anything.

Room service knocks and I jolt from the noise. We put out our cigarettes and David unlatches and answers the door in the nude. He comes back with the bottle, and we pop it open, taking turns holding it by the neck while we drink. He brings me an Ativan from my purse, taking one for himself. I grab the room service menu and crush the tablet as we watch the video again.

I think of my sister's baby and how once a life is gone, it's gone. How we take risks without realizing they are risks, exactly, how death can come for us at any moment. The pain in my tit lingers and I think of the baby I know is already inside me. I touch my stomach when I watch the man on the screen die.

And the man on the screen says *Mamamamamamamama*.

And the man on the screen says *Oh god, oh god, oh god, UGH. Se-se-se-se-se-se-se.*

And the man on the screen kicks and kicks his legs, and then kicks his legs one final time.

ACKNOWLEDGEMENTS

Thank you to Amanda McNeil, Juliet Escoria, Ben Fama, Tyler Gof Barton, Steven Arcieri, B.R. Yeager, Richard Chiem, Cory Bennett, Michael Seidlinger, and Asha Doré.

Thank you to Tom Spanbauer.

Thank you to my best friend and mentor Elizabeth Ellen.

Thank you to my husband.

Thank you to my child for being the greatest gift.

NOTES

- "Who's Afraid of a Funeral Pyre?" first appeared in *The Nervous Breakdown* as "Prize."
- "Joan Jumps into the Sea" was published in *The Offing*.
- "Cat World" was published in *Guernica*.
- "Grace" was published in *Guernica*.
- "Dead to Me" was published *Adroit Journal*.
- "Thank You, Lauren Greenfield" was published in *HARSH Magazine*.
- "We Are Sharp Edges Bumping up Against Each Other" first appeared in *Doestoyevsky Wannabe's Casette 94 Collection*.
- "Livestream" first appeared on *Joyland*.
- "Off Screen I Ache" first appeared as "Anatomy of a Mouth" in *Entropy Magazine*.
- "Survivalist" was published in the *Denver Quarterly*.
- "Unsolved Mysteries" first appeared as "Linsey" in *Rabble Lit*.
- "I Live in A World Where Men With Money Want to Take Away My Wife" first appeared in *Always Crashing*.
- "Summer Thighs" was published in *Tarpaulin Sky*.
- "Community Property" was published in *Wohe Lit*.
- "Nothing But the Night Birds" first appeared as "The Wasp" In *Blunderbuss Magazine*.
- "Charlton Heston Played John the Baptist But I Remember Him as Jesus" was published in *Hobart Pulp*.

- "Deathwish 006" was published in *Nailed Magazine*.
- "Satanism" was published in *Hobart Pulp*.
- "Room Service" was published in *New York Tyrant*.

ABOUT THE AUTHOR

ELLE NASH is the author of *Deliver Me, Nudes, Gag Reflex*, and *Animals Eat Each Other*. Her short stories and essays appear in *Guernica, The Nervous Breakdown, Literary Hub, The Fanzine, Volume 1 Brooklyn, New York Tyrant* and elsewhere. She is a founding editor of *Witch Craft Magazine* and a fiction editor at both *Hobart Pulp* and *Expat Literary Journal*. @saderotica